Past Secrets
Present Danger

Rain City Tales Book Two

Brent Archer

Edited by Delilah Devlin
Cover Design by Nia Morgan

*For Greg, Elle, Delilah, Luke, Maia, Tracy, and the Roses
with love and gratitude.*

ACKNOWLEDGEMENTS

Thanks to Delilah Devlin and Elle James
for the advice and support!

Author's Note

Check out Brent Archer's other stories:

Rain City Tales
The Officer's Siren (Book 1)
Past Secrets Present Danger (Book 2)
I'm Yours (Book 3)
The Wedding Weekend (Book 4)
Mitch's Men (Book 4.5)
Saving Parker (Book 5)
Song of Salvation (Book 6)
Memories of Coromandel (Book 7)
Blaze of Cortez (Book 8) – Coming in 2024

Black Rock Cult Series
Rediscovering Todd (Book 1)
Hiding Hayden (Book 2) – Coming in 2024
Dragging Marshall (Book 3) – Coming in 2025

Stand-Alone Stories
Throuple Honey

For other works by Brent Archer and release dates on
upcoming new stories, visit
www.brentarcher.net

Follow and Like Brent on Facebook
and come visit his Instagram.
facebook.com/brent.archer.186
instagram.com/brent_archer_writer

PROLOGUE

THE WAIL OF a siren sounded from the bedside table. With a glance at his lover's cell, Roger Matthews groaned in protest when his boyfriend, Officer Paul Tomlinson, rose from between his legs, leaving his aching erection high and drying.

"It's work. I have to take this." Paul frowned. "Sorry, babe."

"But this is the first time we've had a chance to make love, between my late nights and your early mornings." Roger sat against the headboard, his cock rapidly deflating. "My balls are going to turn blue."

Paul chuckled as he reached for the phone and touched the screen. "Officer Tomlinson here." He listened intently then rolled off the bed with his phone still pressed against his ear. "I'll be there as fast as I can." He glanced at Roger. "You owe me, Lynch." He touched the screen and ended the call.

Crossing his arms over his chest, Roger watched his lover set his phone on the dresser and rapidly pull on his boxer briefs, the bright green striking against his umber skin. He did his best to track his withering stare on Paul.

Not making eye contact with Roger, Paul continued to

dress. Another interrupted lovemaking session. This one had been instigated by Paul as yet another deflection when Roger had asked about his childhood. After a year and a half, Roger still knew very little about Paul's beginnings, though he knew Paul wasn't from Seattle, and something major must have happened between him and his family to erect such an impenetrable wall.

Paul finally faced him as he buttoned his uniform shirt. "I'm sorry, babe. Really." He moved to the gun safe and spun the combination.

"This is a bad sign, you know." Roger constantly wondered how they'd make it long-term if Paul didn't trust him enough to confide whatever had happened to estrange him from his family.

Paul cocked his head as he opened the heavy, metal door. "In what way?"

"I have a presentation…" Roger glanced at the clock noting the time as two in the morning, "…in seven hours, and you're leaving me unfulfilled. I'm going to end up being a raging bitch."

"Is this an important one?" Paul checked to see if the gun was loaded and snapped the chamber shut.

Roger rubbed at his temples. "It's the software proposal. With the company's expansion into New Zealand, I need to convince the directors to purchase a really expensive accounting system so I can better report on the—"

Chuckling, Paul closed the safe and slipped his gun into its holster. "Anyway, I'll make it up to you. Dinner tonight. Promise."

Roger arched an eyebrow. "Wow, didn't let me come and cut me off. There better be more than dinner involved here, mister."

With a wink, Paul climbed onto the bed and planted a kiss in the middle of Roger's bare chest. "You'll do great. I'll make sure all your needs are met tonight. Promise." Then he pressed a kiss against Roger's lips. "I love you, babe."

With a heavy sigh, Roger pulled Paul into an embrace and kissed his neck. Whatever had happened, Paul always found a way to get out of discussing anything to do with his time before arriving in Seattle. "I love you, too. Go get in your squad car and save the city. What is it this time?"

With a huff, Paul pulled back. "We're taking the *cruiser* to raid a homeless shelter. The staff are beating gay kids and throwing them out into the night without their stuff or any means of keeping warm."

Shaking his head, Roger let Paul go. "What's wrong with them? They're supposed to be helping people."

"I know," Paul said darkly, anger burning in his eyes. "I gotta go." He grabbed his hat off of the dresser and strode from the bedroom.

With a puff of breath, Roger sank back onto the pillow. So much for his romantic morning.

CHAPTER ONE

R OGER PACED THE carpeted floor of his office at Herrington, Fisher, and Scalione. The accounting professional he'd hired as a temp hadn't shown up for work. He'd been counting on her help preparing the presentation to the firm's partners. His phone buzzed. He slipped it from his pants pocket and scanned the screen. An unfamiliar local number appeared. After swiping ACCEPT, Roger brought the phone to his ear. "Hi, this is Roger."

"Hello, Mr. Matthews, this is Claire Underwood. I'm calling from Accounting Professionals Limited. How are you this morning?"

With a frown, Roger glanced at the clock on the wall. Ten-twenty, and no sign of the temp. "Well, I've got a huge presentation in ten minutes, and Sherry hasn't made it into the office this morning."

"Unfortunately, that's what I'm calling about."

Claire paused, and he heard the shuffling of papers.

Roger's stomach tightened. This software meant less stress, a new assistant, and more time at home with Paul, especially important since they'd just decided to move in together.

"Sherry won't be continuing this assignment. Apparently, someone named Marsha Fisher had a verbal altercation with her, and Sherry now refuses to return."

Roger closed his eyes and let out a long breath. "Great." With the presentation looming and Marsha being one of the people he had to convince to spend fifty grand on a new system, having no assistant would make his job even harder.

"She made very clear she enjoyed working with you, however." She paused, and Roger heard the tapping of a keyboard in the background. "I regret also to inform you that we won't be able to provide another temporary employee for your firm. Sherry is the fourth accountant in a two-month period to complain of poor treatment by Ms. Fisher, and we have a strict policy regarding the treatment of our professionals."

With a sigh, Roger crossed to his desk and sat in the chair. "I understand. I can't do anything about Marsha since she's one of the partners. Thanks for your call."

"Good luck, Mr. Matthews. If you are ever looking for other employment, please don't hesitate to let us know." The call ended with two beeps, and Roger slipped the phone into his pocket again. Damn it. He'd actually liked Sherry and had hoped to offer her the assistant position if the three directors approved the proposals in his presentation.

William Herrington strode through the door. A tall, handsome man with flecks of silver in his dark hair, his boss wore a dark suit with a crisp white shirt and a sea-green tie, matching his intense eyes. "Roger, we're ready for you." His eyebrows rose. "Why the long face?"

Roger set his elbows on the desk and ran his hands over his face. "Sherry isn't coming back. Marsha unloaded on her yesterday, and now the agency won't send anyone else."

Herrington's brow furrowed as he closed the door. "Damn it. I know this is putting you in a tough spot. I'll have a word with her."

"Maybe wait until *after* she approves spending the money on the new system?" He looked over his fingertips. "If I don't get approval from all three of you, I can't spend the money, and we really need this with the Auckland office coming online."

Taking a seat across from Roger, Herrington fixed him with a stare. "True, but we also need to get you some permanent help. This string of temps and your late nights aren't sustainable. I'm well aware you could easily get another job with less demands on your time. I don't want to lose you."

"I'd appreciate some more help, and so would my relationship with Paul." Roger puffed out another sigh, thinking of their interrupted session earlier in the morning. "We'll get through this—even without Sherry's help. The presentation is compelling."

"You'll have my full support. Don't worry. I'll make sure you'll have a substantial raise after we're up and running." Herrington pushed up from his seat. "Let's get this over with."

Roger stood and followed his boss to the conference room. Seated around the large table were Marsha Fisher, the Director of Marketing and Branding, with her straw-colored straight hair and stern, humorless face, and Angelica Scalione, the Director of Operations and IT, with her long, dark hair and wide smile. His boss, William Herrington, CEO and CFO, sat at the head of the conference table and motioned for Roger to sit at the other end.

With the three directors staring impassively at him, Roger felt like he was facing an inquisition.

Marsha's gravelly voice cut across the silence, "So, Billy, here, tells me you need a bigger accounting system."

Shooting her a warning glare, Herrington pursed his lips. "Marsha."

To head off the usual divergence into bickering about the inappropriateness of directors using his first name in front of staff, let alone a nickname, Roger turned to the open laptop and quickly pulled up the PowerPoint presentation he'd prepared. Though he'd intended for Sherry to run the technical part of the program while he spoke, he'd make do and try to act like he'd planned to present solo from the get-go. The large screen on the wall lit up, and the bickering partners turned their attention to the presentation.

Roger clicked on the first slide. "As we continue to grow and expand our programs and marketing, we need to be able to adequately account for each initiative. Currently, our system only allows two ways to slice and dice the numbers."

Angelica leaned forward. "The reporting I've asked for seems to work."

Roger suppressed a wince, recalling several late nights he'd spent away from Paul preparing those reports. "What I generate for you must first be pulled out of our current software and manipulated in Excel. The process is time-consuming, and as we continue to grow, will become even more burdensome. The software I've researched and recommended in my e-mail will produce ready-made reports quickly generated to present to funders as well as give you exactly what you need to track costs and revenue for each individual initiative, both here and in Auckland."

Herrington nodded. "Yes, the costs we save in Roger's time and whomever we hire to support the controller position will pay for the software."

Raising an eyebrow, Marsha looked from Herrington to Roger. "What do you mean, *whomever we hire*? What happened to Cynthia?"

"*Sherry*," Roger began, frowning, "decided not to return."

"Oh?" Marsha leaned back. "Lost another one, eh? If you can't keep temporary staff, why should we hire you someone permanent?"

With his blood boiling, Roger took a moment, hoping Herrington would respond. When his red-faced boss didn't come to his rescue, Roger took the bull by the horns as he remembered the recruiter's offer when she told him Sherry wasn't coming back. Though trying to remain professional, his words came out clipped. "There seems to be some hostility toward my staff that the temporary employees find inappropriate and completely untenable." He leveled a stern glare at Marsha. "Sherry didn't come in this morning because of an altercation she had yesterday with you."

A smirk spread across her face. "I didn't like her anyway."

Roger pressed forward, knowing full well he could get a job anywhere, even if he got fired for insubordination. Marsha Fisher didn't scare him in the slightest. "Because you've pushed out so many accountants, the agency will no longer work with us. At this rate, you won't have an accounting department, and you'll likely have the Department of Revenue and the IRS breathing down your neck when you fail to file your tax payments—never mind your staff jumping ship because they aren't being paid."

The smirk disappeared from Marsha's face, replaced by a tight-lipped frown. "What's your point?"

All attempts at remaining calm were abandoned as he zeroed in on the number one problem he faced at Herrington, Fisher, and Scalione. "My *point* is, if you drive away the next person I hire, I'm going with them. There's a huge shortage of good accounting professionals in this city, and you've burned through four in the last two months."

"I'm well aware of the shortage." Marsha crossed her arms and gave Roger a pointed stare. "If we give you this software, you'll stay?"

"I'll stay if you approve my recommendation—and if you back off of whomever I hire." Refusing to blink, Roger pressed his advantage. "If you have complaints or issues, you can go through me, which is much more appropriate than skewering my staff."

An expression of what Roger could only describe as admiration spread across Marsha's face as she turned to Herrington. "This one has balls, Billy. About time you hired someone who can stand up for himself."

Herrington sighed. "Angelica, what do you think?"

"I think we'd better give him his software." She grinned at Roger. "I was already a yes from the excellent research you provided to us last week."

With a nod, Herrington turned to Marsha. "Well?"

"Yup." She pushed her chair back and stood. "If there's nothing else, I have work to do." She gave a brief glance at Roger that seemed to say *well done* and marched from the room.

Roger's confusion bubbled through his anger at the marketing director. After she'd ambled down the hallway and turned the corner, he gazed at the other two partners. "What just happened here?"

With a small laugh, Angelica stood, gathering the papers in front of her and her water glass. "I think you impressed her. She respects people willing stand up to her and call her out." She arched an eyebrow. "Just don't make a habit of it."

"Sorry, I don't know what got into me." He fought the warmth rushing into his cheeks as he realized how insubordinate he'd been toward one of the partners. Fearing he'd face the music with his direct boss, he tore his eyes from Angelica and settled his gaze on Herrington.

The senior partner grinned. "Son, you got your software."

"HEY, BABE. HOW'S your day going?"

Paul's tired voice made him smile.

"I've certainly had a day," Roger said as he closed his computer and lifted his backpack from beneath the desk. "Got the software and the okay to hire someone."

"I knew you could do it." His boyfriend yawned into the phone.

Roger moved to the door and grabbed his coat. "You okay?"

"Yeah. Can't wait to get home to you."

Warmth spread through Roger. He shrugged into the jacket, jockeying the cell between his hands. "You're such a charmer."

"I mean it. You did some wonderful things to me this morning before I had to leave."

"Yeah, that was kind of rude," he said with a crooked grin, thinking about where Paul's mouth had been when his phone went off. He glanced down the hall, relieved to see only darkened doorways. Tonight, he'd make a clean escape. At five-thirty, the firm was a ghost town, and this was the earliest he'd left the office in weeks.

"I promised to make it up to you," Paul murmured. "A bite at the place in Ravenna?"

"You mean the brewpub where you play pool with the Templetons?" Roger's mouth watered at the thought of one of their signature meat pies served with a mountain of tater tots.

"That's the one. I'll come by and pick you up. Finished for today?" The excitement in his lover's voice was unmistakable.

"Got my coat on, and I'm heading for the door." He pushed the marker next to his name to OUT and left the reception area. "Are you coming in the truck or the squad car?"

"You mean the cruiser?" Paul's voice lowered, his clipped words reflecting the annoyance from earlier in the morning.

A smirk spread across his face. "No, I said squad car." After their interrupted lovemaking, he relished pushing his favorite button. Served Paul right for leaving him with blue balls this morning.

Blowing out a puff of air on the other end of the phone, Paul cleared his throat. "*Anyway*, I'll come in the truck."

The elevator door opened, and Roger stepped into the carriage, pressing the button for the lobby. "You will if you play your cards right," he quipped.

There was a moment's silence. "In the truck?"

The breathy quality of Paul's voice sent heat straight toward his groin. "Anywhere you want. Just so you don't leave me high and dry like you did this morning."

Paul chuckled. "Okay, I promise. You come first. *After* we eat."

The elevator came to a halt, and Roger strode into the lobby. The tall, lean concierge was just slipping on his jacket.

"Then I'll see you out in front of the building. I'm in the lobby now." Roger gave the young man a wave and settled himself onto one of the couches beside the revolving door.

"See you in ten." The call ended with a double beep.

The concierge grabbed his backpack and paused at the couch. "Hi, Roger. How did your day go?"

"Pretty well, thanks. Merrick, right?" The young man had replaced the long-time concierge, Horatio, and Roger constantly struggled to remember his name.

The young man smiled. "Correct. Merrick Hamilton, at your service." He bowed his lanky frame.

Laughing, Roger extended his hand. "Roger Matthews."

"Right. Isn't Sherry working for you? She's the accounting temp, right?"

With a grumble, Roger shook his head. "She refused to come back. Hopefully, she found a better opportunity."

"That's why I didn't see her this morning. Kind of leaves you in a bind, though. I'll keep my ears open. You never know what kind of connections are out there."

Roger glanced out the window, looking for Paul's rig but not seeing it. "I'd appreciate that. Whoever I hire has to have a thick skin when it comes to the partners."

Chuckling, Merrick shook his head. "Just one of the partners from what I've heard about your firm."

"True." A black Ford truck pulled into the load zone in front of the building, and Roger jumped to his feet. He couldn't help the smile spreading across his lips at the sight of Paul waving from the open truck window. "That's my ride. See you in the morning."

Merrick waved and held open the glass door. "Have a great evening."

Roger trotted to the truck and pulled open the door.

"That was quick." The sight of his boyfriend decked out in a royal blue button-up shirt and grey slacks made him want to skip dinner and go straight home. Only his uniform looked sexier on him. Roger climbed in and stretched across the console, pressing his lips against his lover's.

As he sat back, Paul whistled. "Damn, I love how you kiss me. Always makes my day."

Slipping on his seatbelt and pressing the window control, Roger settled into the seat and laid his other hand on Paul's thigh. "I love everything you do to me." He squeezed the muscular leg, then drifted his fingers up to the substantial bulge in Paul's trousers, causing a stirring under the fabric. "Especially with this."

Paul pushed the gearshift into first and pulled into traffic. "Babe, if I wasn't so hungry right now, I'd take you home and do all kinds of things to you."

With a final squeeze on the chubbing dick, which elicited a grunt from his lover, Roger retreated his hand down to the warm, hard thigh. "Don't eat too much of the fried stuff. You'll crash by the time we get home and spoil all the plans I have for you."

Chuckling, Paul turned left onto the carpool entrance to Interstate Five. "Don't worry. I'm looking forward to pleasuring you this evening." He shifted into fifth gear and settled his hands on the steering wheel. "Tell me about your day. You got the software?"

Roger settled back against his seat. "Yup, and you wouldn't believe how."

"Oh, yeah?" Paul gave a sideways glance and a little

smirk. "Did you have to blow Herrington?"

Roger rolled his eyes. "Seriously?"

Paul burst out laughing. "Come on, babe. He's a total hot daddy-type. What do the boys call guys like him?"

"Straight, and old enough to be my father." An image of the tall man sitting at his desk flashed into Roger's mind. He shook his head before he continued that train of thought.

Paul slapped the steering wheel with one of his meaty hands. "Silver foxes."

Widening his eyes in mock horror, Roger stared at his boyfriend, dramatically bringing a hand over his mouth and gasping. "Are you having an affair with my boss? I *knew* you wanted him. Do you bottom for him?"

Paul shot him a glance through narrowed eyes before returning his attention to the road. "Ew. Just, ew."

Crossing his arms victoriously, Roger smirked. "That's what I thought. I don't need images in my head of my boss in any other capacity or position than *as my employer*, thank you very much. Now, do you want to hear about my software or not?"

"I'd rather look at your hardware," he grumbled, "but since I'm driving, you'd better just tell me about your day."

With a laugh, Roger glanced out the window as they cruised over the Ship Canal Bridge toward the University District. "I got in Marsha's face, and instead of exploding at me, she gave me this approving look and agreed to, not only the software, but hiring another person, full time and permanent."

"Wow, babe. That's amazing." He gave Roger a grin. "You just had to tell her she's a bitch."

"I actually would have preferred, in some ways, that she fired me. It's going to be quite a chore to get someone in to help." He thought about the woman at the temp agency. "Sherry didn't come back after three days in the office because of Marsha, and now the agency won't send anyone else. I told Marsha that if I lose one more person because of her, I'd quit."

"Good for you. Keep those directors in line." Paul maneuvered the truck around a slow-moving car and merged into the exit lane for Northeast Sixty-Fifth Street. "What's your plan? More late nights?"

"At this point, I'm not sure. I want to be home with you, not pulling late nights." Roger considered his predicament, mentally scrolling through the accounting professionals he knew. "I wonder if Clark has any bandwidth to come in and help me."

"Clark Adamson? Doesn't he work at that non-profit on Capitol Hill. I've sent several gay street kids over there. Haven't seen them since, so Clark's place must be helping those boys and girls." Paul's grip tightened on the steering wheel as his jaw clenched for a moment. Flipping on his blinker, he turned the truck onto Sixty-Fifth.

"You don't just send them over. You pretty much pick them up off the street and drive them." Roger regarded his lover curiously. "Speaking of which, what happened with the shelter you got called away to raid?"

"Just like we thought. Found a room full of backpacks and clothes." Paul's grip tightened again. "It won't be easy to get everything back to the kids," Paul huffed. "We have the sign-in records. Names, but no descriptions."

Warming at the sight of his lover's passion for his work, Roger rubbed Paul's leg. "It's a big deal to you, helping these kids."

Paul shrugged, his grip still tight. "I'm paying back." He brought the truck to a quick halt as the light changed at University Avenue. Turning to Roger, he leaned forward and placed a kiss on his lips.

Roger mused on the common refrain. He'd make a comment or ask a question about the homeless gay kids Paul helped on a daily basis. Paul tightened up and evaded the conversation away from anything to do with his own past or why he felt so strongly about helping them. He'd only say he was paying back. When pressed to elaborate, Paul would either kiss him, or cross his arms and shut down the conversation with a stern glare or leave the room.

"Now, now." Roger chuckled, pulling back from his boyfriend. "I don't want to distract you while you're driving. You could get a ticket for that."

Laughing, Paul turned and faced the traffic light. "True. I should lead by example."

"Correct." He tugged his cell from his pocket. "I'm going to send Clark a quick text. Doesn't hurt to ask."

The light changed, and Paul stomped on the accelerator, pushing Roger back into the seat.

"Okay, speed racer. Dial it back." He slapped Paul's thigh. "Example, remember?"

With another laugh, Paul shifted into second, slowing

their acceleration. "We're almost to the pub anyway." He turned onto a side street and found a spot in the neighborhood to park.

Roger tapped at the screen of his cell, sending his friend Clark a quick message, asking if he had any daytime free. Pocketing the phone, he released himself from the seatbelt and pushed open the door.

Placing a hand on Roger's leg, Paul stopped him from getting out. "Let's make out before we go inside."

"Naughty boy," Roger admonished. "It's still daylight outside."

Paul shrugged. "We're in a secluded spot. I'll blow you in the truck."

A surge of desire coursed through Roger and his cock swelled in his slacks. "I thought you didn't want to come until after dinner?"

Paul wiggled his eyebrows. "I'll work you up to the main event."

"Much as I want to, I don't think Seb wants to see Officer Friendly jutting from your trousers." Roger cupped his hand around Paul's crotch, squeezing the hardening shaft through the fabric between his thumb and index finger. "I'd rather get a bite, and *then* take you home to bed."

Paul sighed. "Okay, you win. Serves me right for leaving you wanting. Your place or mine?"

Roger grinned. "After next week, you won't have to ask that question." Paul asking him to move in had been one of the happiest moments of their relationship. He'd given his boyfriend an enthusiastic yes at the invitation.

He hoped it foreshadowed a deepening of their connection. Sharing a home would certainly test their compatibility, although Roger already spent most evenings there anyway, whether Paul was at work or not. So, there seemed little reason to continue wasting money on two places. He'd pay Paul half of the mortgage payment as rent and share other expenses, helping them both out. Seattle wasn't exactly cheap, after all.

Paul's stomach picked that moment to rumble loudly.

Lifting the officer's hand to his lips, Roger chuckled and kissed the knuckles. "You must be starving."

"Okay, okay. Let's get some food." He laid his hand on Roger's neck and pulled him into an embrace. Their lips met. After lingering a moment, Paul broke the kiss and let his hand drift down to Roger's shoulder. "I love you."

A smile inched across Roger's face as the tingling warmth of their affection warmed his lips. "I love you, too."

The pub teemed with people as they stepped inside, and Roger thought the restaurant seemed overly crowded for a mid-week evening. Paul navigated his way through the sea of chairs, holding Roger's hand and steering him to a small table not far from the pool table, where Fred waved his arms in animated conversation with Alex and Sarah Templeton.

"Not sitting at the bar this evening, gents?" The bartender, Seb, approached the table with two coasters and tossed the disks onto the table top.

Paul grinned. "No room. How's married life treating you?"

"I think your buxom Italian wife disappointed all the women and over half the men in this place when she caught you," Roger joined in.

Seb laughed. "Emily's amazing. I'm still marveling at how awesome she is." He leaned in. "Although, just between the three of us, I could do without the jogging outfits she comes up with. Love is blind, though, eh?"

As Seb moved to another table, Fred hurried over. "Paul, good that you're here. Alex and Sarah challenged me to a game, and I need my partner."

Eyeing his co-worker, Paul crossed his arms. "What's the matter?" he asked, his tone wry. "Your pool-shark buddy, Mike, not available?"

Fred's eyes widened. "It was just that one time, I swear. You were out of town, and I was in a bind."

"That's not what Sarah said," Roger piped up. He loved joining in the teasing interplay between Paul and his boss, and loved even more the fact Paul's friends and fellow officers had accepted him so readily into their circle. "She told me you constantly beg Mike to come play."

Paul shifted his gaze from Roger to Fred. "Is this true?" he asked with exaggerated dismay and indignation.

Swinging his gaze toward Sarah and Alex, Fred glared at the couple. The Templetons exchanged glances and shrugged while smothering smiles.

Officer Jason Lynch and his husband Mike Bryant wove their way to Roger and Paul's table.

Mike's goofy smile lit up his face. "Did someone mention my name?"

Stifling a laugh, Roger sat back and watched the officers bicker about who was entitled to play and how often Mike was cutting in on Paul's gig. Seb bustled over and planted his hands on his hips. "All right, boys. If you don't cool it," he said, winking at Roger, "I'll have to call the cops."

The room filled with the roar of laughter from the three officers. Jason and Mike took the two extra seats at the table, and Roger handed his menu over to the pair.

"I'm ready to order, Seb," Roger said.

Seb pulled his pad from his apron. "Shoot."

"The steak and cheddar pie with a mound of tater tots." He glanced at the beer list. "And...a bottle of Roger's Pilsner."

Mike chuckled next to Roger. "I'll have the same, except I want a ginger beer."

Seb nodded. "Paul?"

As his boyfriend and Jason ordered, Roger cast Fred a bemused grin. The poor guy was desperate for Paul to go shoot a game of pool with the Templetons, and Paul was purposefully taking his time, being indecisive about his food and drink order.

When Seb finally left the table, Fred plunked down between Paul and Jason. "Seriously, are you going to help me out, Paul?" He glanced across the table at Mike. "I'm sure there's someone else here who'd play if you don't want to."

Paul leaned toward Roger. "What do you think, babe?"

"Let Mike play." Roger grinned. "The game'll be over in about five minutes."

Another roar of laughter erupted from the table, although this time Fred didn't join in. He looked like a spoiled child whose favorite toy had been stolen away.

Taking pity on him, Roger turned to Fred. "Just kidding. Go shoot one game." Roger raised his index finger and waved it in front of Paul. "*One* game. You have commitments after we're done eating."

Heat burned through the look Paul shot him as he pushed himself to his feet. "Okay, Fred. You heard the boss. One game."

"Commitments?" Jason looked between them.

Mike chuckled and reached his hand under the table. "Commitments."

Eyes widening, Jason stared at his husband. "Oh. *Commitments.*"

With a shake of his head, Fred led Paul to the far side of the bar.

Seb brought their drinks, and, with a glance at the pool table, carried Paul's over to him.

Jason's easy demeanor evaporated, and Roger wondered at the sudden change.

"So, Roger, what have you been up to lately? We haven't seen you out in a while." Mike took a sip of his ginger beer.

"We're purchasing a new accounting system at the firm. Kind of exciting, but it means I'll be working even more than I am now, at least at the beginning." He lifted his beer. "We're short-handed right now."

Jason snorted. "Is your work running out of money or something?"

Tilting his head to the right, Roger furrowed his brow in confusion as he studied Jason. "Why do you say that?"

"Well, I'd think marketing firms aren't doing so well these days." He took a long draw from his pint of lager.

"No, actually, we're doing pretty well. Marketing is only part of the business model. We're doing so well that we've opened an office in New Zealand." He considered his lover's beat partner. Ever since he'd been reassigned to Paul, because Fred had been promoted, Jason had been unpredictably sullen and moody. Paul had put it down to not adjusting well to change, but it seemed like there was something else going on.

Jason sniffed. "I hear you're moving in with Paul."

Grateful for a topic that brought him joy, Roger grinned. "Yeah. Paul asked me to live with him. I think it's a good decision for both of us."

"Is that so?" Jason scowled as he took another drink of his beer.

Mike gave Jason an elbow in the ribs and fixed him with a pointed stare. "Isn't that great news?" With a smile, Mike turned to Roger. "Sounds like a big step."

With a shrug, Roger lifted his pint. "It is, but I think it's one we've been building toward. We've been together over a year and a half." He took a sip then set the glass on the table, returning his gaze to the sulking officer. "Is there something wrong, Jason?"

"Why do say that?" He sneered and imitated Roger's tone from a moment ago.

Lodging his tongue against his upper teeth, Roger narrowed his eyes. "Do you have a problem with me moving in with Paul?"

Mike's mouth firmed into a straight line.

Jason's gaze locked with Roger's. "Paul's a nice guy, and I think people could easily take advantage of him. Are you moving in with him just to get free rent or something?"

Not only disapproving, Jason's frown felt downright hostile.

"What?" The question hit Roger like a freight train, and he wondered if he'd heard correctly.

"Jason, knock it off. What the hell is wrong with you?" Mike hissed as he shot his husband a glare.

"I just want to be sure my friend isn't making a big mistake. Seems like every time we're out, Paul's paying your way." Jason leaned forward, his features hardening. "The last thing Paul needs is a freeloader taking advantage of him."

Mike's eyes widened in horror. "Jason!"

Roger stood, his temper boiling over. "Well, it's good to know what you think of me and where I stand." He grabbed his and Paul's coats.

Standing, Mike placed a hand on his shoulder. "Roger, wait."

"For what? Another insult?" Shrugging off Mike's grip, he turned back to glare at Jason. The big, bad intimidating cop game Paul's co-worker was playing didn't scare Roger in the slightest. "You know, asshole, I've had a very good job for a long time, well before I ever met Paul. I've had to stand on my own two feet since I was a teenager, paying my way through college, because I didn't want to be a burden on my parents."

Jason glared at him. "But now you've got a meal ticket."

Shaking his head, Roger's voice hardened as he met the other man's glare head on. "I'll be sharing the mortgage payment equally as my part of the rent. I pay for myself, Jason Lynch. Just because you don't happen to have your nose buried in my ledger books doesn't mean that I don't. And, not that I have to prove my value to you or anyone else, but I'm getting a substantial *raise* at work because I know how to stand up to bullying jackasses like you."

He left a wide-eyed, gaping Jason and a seriously blushing Mike and stalked across the room.

As he approached the pool tables, Paul bent over and lined up his shot. He thrust the cue forward and smacked the eight-ball clean into the side pocket. A wide grin spread over his face, but it immediately evaporated when he noticed Roger.

Not trusting his voice, Roger handed Paul his coat and hitched his thumb toward the door.

Cocking his head, Paul slipped on the jacket. "What's wrong, babe? We're leaving without dinner?"

"Damned right we are." Roger fumed, voice trembling in rage.

Fred skirted the pool table and stood next to Paul. "Are you okay, Roger?"

With a shake of his head, he returned his glare to Paul. "If you want to stay, I'll get a Lyft to my apartment. You can join me there when you're done."

Seb hurried over to them. "Everything okay, guys?"

Before Paul could answer, Roger spun to face the bartender. "Are the pies done?"

With a bewildered frown, Seb nodded. "I was just about to bring them over to your table."

"Can you put them in a box?" Roger fished in his pocket and handed over his credit card. He wanted to yell over at Jason to notice he was the one paying for dinner, but controlled his anger enough not to embarrass himself further or make any more of a scene than he already was.

"Uh, yeah. Give me a minute." Seb hustled away toward the kitchen.

Paul's hands gripped Roger's shoulders. "Tell me what happened."

"I won't be spending another minute in Officer Lynch's presence." He narrowed his eyes. "Ever."

Glancing over Roger's shoulder, Paul shot a confused stare at the table where Mike and Jason sat, but Roger refused to spare a backward glance. Returning his attention to Roger, Paul cupped his cheek. "Okay, we'll talk about it when we get home." He placed a soft kiss on Roger's lips and turned to his pool partner. "Good thing I won the game for you, Fred. We gotta go."

Fred stared at Roger, obvious concern etched on his features, but he didn't say anything.

Seb returned, handing the card, a pen, and the payment slip to Roger. He passed the bag with their dinner to Paul. "Take care, guys. Hope we see you again soon."

"We'll see," Roger grumbled as he handed the slip and pen back to Seb.

Leaving Seb confused with the signed ticket and a heavy frown, Roger strode to the door of the pub. Mike stood and tried to get his attention, but Roger purposefully ignored him. Though he knew Mike wasn't to blame for what Jason had said, he didn't want to give Jason another chance to insult him. Besides, when Paul found out what he'd implied, all hell would break loose. He didn't want Seb to *really* have to call the police.

Paul hurried to his side after they exited the restaurant. "Babe, what happened? What did Lynch say?"

"Please, just take me home." Roger stopped next to the truck and stared through the tinted window.

Sighing, Paul unlocked the door and held it open for his boyfriend. Once Roger sat and belted up, Paul handed him the take-out containers and shut the door, trotting around the other side of the truck and getting in. He started the ignition and placed his hand on Roger's thigh after pulling out of the parking spot and onto the neighborhood streets. The firm warmth of his hand eased some of his anger, but he still fumed.

Roger stared straight ahead as they turned onto Sixty-Fifth. The cell in his pocket vibrated, and he reached for it. A message from Clark filled the screen.

I can meet you at your office tomorrow morning. Your Mkt Dir doesn't scare me. A smile emoticon with devil horns grinned evilly at him.

He snorted derisively. *At least something good came out of this evening.*

CHAPTER TWO

THE ALARM WOKE ROGER at five-thirty. Even after a good night's sleep wrapped in the arms of the man who loved him, Roger still burned. How could that shithead Jason Lynch say that he was a freeloader? Where the hell had that come from anyway?

A loud snore emanated from the man he was still cuddled up against. Paul's umber skin contrasted beautifully against the pale white of Roger's arm. Roger ran his fingers through the tight swirls of dark hair covering Paul's broad chest, enjoying the soft skin and the tickle as his fingers progressed along tight abs and into a neatly trimmed bush.

As Roger's fingers lit across the morning erection poking from the sheets, Paul sucked in a deep breath. "Mornin', babe."

"Hey there. Sorry to wake you," he said, holding back a smile as he lazily stroked Paul's cock. After he was certain he had his attention, he leaned forward and gave him a kiss.

Paul's hands captured Roger's head and held him in their lip lock. The grip slackened as Roger grazed his palm across the tip of Paul's cock and then held the shaft in his fingers, alternating between gently squeezing and stroking along the sensitive skin.

With a gasp, Paul's hands fell to his side, and he broke the kiss. "Oh, babe, you know how to touch me."

Keeping his hand on Paul's cock, Roger scooted onto his stomach and reached over to the small bedside table where a bottle of lube sat, left there from their lovemaking the night before. The light ache in his ass and the warmth swelling in his chest reminded him of their intense session. He snatched the bottle, turned onto his side, and popped open the top, pausing to squirt a liberal amount onto Paul's erection. After closing the top and tossing the bottle onto the pillow behind him, Roger spread the liquid over each nook and cranny of Paul's hardness. A loud moan escaped his lover's lips as Roger continued to stroke, increasing his rhythm.

"What about you, babe?" Paul panted while his knees moved upward and spread.

"I've got what I want in my hand." He gave a squeeze before resuming his rhythm and increasing his speed. Noting the tightening of Paul's balls and the hardening of the shaft, Roger clamped onto one of Paul's dark nipples with his lips and tongued the sensitive nub.

"Oh, fuck!" Paul screamed, gripping the sheets as his cock pulsed in Roger's hand. Spurt after spurt painted his dark skin with ropes of white liquid.

Roger slowed his stroking, careful not to run his slick hand over the highly sensitive head. He knew from prior experience that Paul bucked like a bronco after his orgasm if Roger worked the tip. Still, a light teasing wouldn't hurt that much. He tickled his fingers just under the ridge of Paul's plum-shaped head.

With a sharp intake of breath, Paul grabbed Roger's wrist while his back arched. "Babe, please."

"Okay, okay. I'll be merciful." He slackened his grip, and Paul let go of his wrist.

"Damn, that was amazing." Paul rolled to his side and planted a kiss on Roger's lips. "I need a nap."

With a laugh, Roger gave Paul one last peck on the cheek and pushed up to sit. "I wish I could join you, but I need to get to work."

"What about you, babe? I'm leaving you high and dry—again." Paul traced a pattern on Roger's back.

Relishing the tender caress, Roger considered calling in sick, but Clark had agreed to meet him at the office, and he couldn't leave his friend to the mercy of Marsha. He sighed. "I wish I could, but I have to meet Clark."

With a groan, Paul wrapped his arm around Roger's waist and pulled him back. "Clark's a big boy. He can handle himself."

Giggling, Roger disentangled himself and scurried off the bed. "You're a bad boy, tempting me like that." His own cock jerked as he raked his gaze over Paul's dark skin still covered in drying semen, the lure of a few more minutes wrapped in his arms calling him back to bed.

Paul rolled onto his stomach, shooting Roger a cheeky grin over his shoulder as he pushed his bubble butt into the air. "You should get back here and spank me."

Resisting the strong urge to jump on the bed and ravage his boyfriend, Roger exhaled a long breath. "Sorry, sweetheart, but I've got to earn a living." His mood soured as Jason's words from the prior evening came back to him. "Wouldn't want a freeloader living here, would you?"

In a flash, Paul sprang from the bed and wrapped his arms around Roger, pulling him tight against his muscular body. "You're *not* a freeloader. He's not getting away with insulting you."

Roger huffed. "You could break his nose for me if you want." He buried his face in the hard pillows of Paul's pecs.

"Listen," Paul said as he held onto Roger's shoulders and pushed him back so their gazes met. "I'm thrilled you agreed to move in with me. Don't let some jealous asshole ruin it for us."

"You are?" Roger eyed his boyfriend, unsure if it was such a wonderful thing if his beat partner didn't approve. Paul had to work with the asshole nearly every day, after all.

"Damned right, I am." Paul spun him around and patted his butt. "Now get into the shower, and I'll make you breakfast." He placed a kiss between Roger's shoulder blades. "Gotta take care of my man."

Warmth spread from the site of the kiss across his back and into his chest. He glanced over his shoulder. "You really love me?"

Paul enveloped him in strong arms. "Crazy about you, babe." His nose and lips nuzzled against Roger's neck. "*Love* isn't a strong enough word."

Wrapping his arms around Paul, Roger gave him a squeeze then stepped from his embrace. "I love you, too."

Reassured by both Paul's words and the tenderness of his hug, he headed for the bathroom and turned on the water in the shower. Holding his hand under the stream, he waited for the water to warm. With Clark coming into the office later in the morning, this should prove to be an interesting day.

THE BUS HEADING into downtown bumped along the potholes on Third Avenue in Belltown. Roger sighed and held onto the overhead bar for the ride. This was one of those mornings where he'd caught a later bus and had to stand. With all the construction going on everywhere in the city, the roads had taken a beating. One of the wettest winters on record also hadn't helped the condition of the streets.

When the bus finally stopped at Union Street, Roger stepped off with the rush of people and ran the block, fighting the driving rain to his office building. Stepping through the revolving door, he waved at Merrick and shook off his dripping coat.

Merrick waved back as Roger approached the desk. "Hi, Roger. Quite a squall outside this morning."

"More than a squall." He wiped his wet hands on the back of his slacks. "I'd be happy if we could have a few days without the rain."

Merrick nodded toward the front window. "I actually like the rain. The more we get, the greener the city stays."

"I suppose that's true." Roger glanced at his phone for the time. "I've got about five minutes before I have to head upstairs. One of my friends is coming to help me out with some accounting work."

"Tall guy with wavy hair and a kind face? Answers to the name of Clark?"

Roger's eyes widened. "How did you know that?"

Wriggling his eyebrows, Merrick grinned. "He arrived about ten minutes ago. Said he was working in your office today." He gave a shrug. "I let him in. He looked on the up-and-up."

With a shake of his head, Roger stared at the young man. "You're amazing."

Merrick gave another shrug, but the grin on his face brightened his features. "Just part of my job."

"Which you are very good at. I'd better get upstairs." He turned and headed toward the elevator bank.

"Have a great day, Roger," Merrick called from behind him.

Roger stopped and turned with a grin. "It should be interesting. Clark doesn't back down when pushed, so I'll be fascinated to see what he does with the difficult director we spoke about yesterday."

Merrick's mischievous grin matched Roger's. "I look forward to hearing about it."

Turning back to the elevators, Roger stepped through one of the open doors and pressed floor twenty. The doors closed, and the empty car gave him a moment to collect his thoughts. He actually worried more about Clark taking Marsha down than he did about Marsha making another accounting professional head for the door. Though tactful in most situations, Clark didn't take crap off of anyone.

The elevator arrived at his floor, and the doors opened with a ding. Roger strode though the hallway and into the reception area to find Clark and Marsha engaged in conversation. A pit opened in Roger's stomach as he worried he was about to witness a huge train wreck.

Marsha's gravelly voice cut across the reception area. "Are you kidding me with this?"

Impassively, Clark shook his head. "Serious as a heart attack."

The marketing director let her head fall back as she roared with laughter.

Roger arched an eyebrow at his friend and was greeted with a slight smirk.

Getting her laughter under control, Marsha's gaze fell onto Roger. "I like your new little helper here." She patted Clark's shoulder and chuckled as she ambled down the hallway and turned the corner.

Stepping to his friend, Roger gave Clark a quick embrace. "What did you say to her?"

"I told her about one of my former clients when I was an independent auditor and their marketing debacle. You know, the one where the marketing firm I did the audit for lost all their client's proof sheets, then substituted the presentation with some hastily drawn images on regular copy paper and told the client they were going for a simple, almost cartoonish feel."

Roger chuckled. "I sort of remember that one, but I don't remember what happened."

"They not only got the contract, but the campaign worked brilliantly." Clark shook his head. "Unfortunately, their books were a disaster."

Elsibeth chuckled from the reception desk. "I've never seen anyone handle her like that."

"I've dealt with folks a lot worse than Marsha Fisher." Clark shrugged. "You just have to find their interests and deflect their attention from you back onto themselves."

Roger crossed his arms and gave Clark an appraising look. "I'll have to remember that about you."

Clark returned the look with a grin. "Shall we get started?"

"Definitely." Roger marked himself in and gave Elsibeth a quick wave as they headed for his office. "We have several goalposts of the integration to figure out before we speak with Herrington."

"How can I help?"

"Let me show you some of the technical specs, and we'll go over the data migration aspect." Roger glanced at the clock over the sign-in board. "We've got a couple hours before Herrington expects us in his office."

ROGER ACCOMPANIED CLARK to the lobby at four o'clock. "Thanks for staying the whole day. I don't think I could have gotten through that planning session without you. You've saved me a late night. I can't remember the last time I was able to leave at four."

"No problem at all." Clark pulled his cell from his pocket and poked at the screen. "I should be able to come in again on Tuesday. I have meetings the rest of the week, and Mondays are a little crazy most of the time."

"I'm grateful for anything you can give me." He gave Clark a hug. "And I get to go home to Paul. He'll be shocked."

Patting his back, Clark broke the embrace and leveled a stern gaze. "Don't let that jerk of a cop devalue you."

Roger jolted. "You mean Paul?"

His brow still furrowed, Clark shook his head. "No, Paul's great. The asshole calling you a freeloader. If you want, I'll go to that pub and break his nose."

With a chuckle, Roger shook his head. "You'd get arrested for assaulting an officer. Besides, he completely outweighs you."

"I'd wait until he was off duty." He pocketed the phone then extended his arms and cracked his knuckles. "And I have a mean left hook."

"I think Paul will take care of it for me." His own cell buzzed, and he fished it from his pants pocket. "Speak of the devil." A flush of warmth settled over Roger as he slid his finger across the screen. "Hey, sweetheart, what's up?"

"I'm just down the block. Can I come see you?" Paul's cheerful voice made Roger smile.

"Believe it or not, I'm actually done for the day."

"Really?" The excitement coming through the phone was infectious.

"Yeah, Clark and I are in the lobby discussing your buddy Jason." Roger gave Clark a wink. "We think he'd look better with a broken nose."

"Don't do anything I'll have to bail you out for," Paul warned. "He was having a bad night."

Roger huffed. "He wasn't the only one."

"I know. Mike ripped him a new one when they got home. He slept on the couch that night."

"Poor baby," Roger spat.

"C'mon, babe. Give him another chance," Paul implored.

Eager for a subject change, Roger sighed. "I'm in the lobby now. If you want to come pick me up, I certainly wouldn't object."

"On my way." The phone beeped twice, and Roger pocketed the cell.

He turned back to Clark. "I'll walk you out." He led the way toward the main entrance.

Clark kept pace with him. "Send a text if things get out of hand with the initial contract. If you're desperate, I can probably juggle something."

Holding the door open, Roger shook his head. "This is in no way a rush job or a disaster. The usual reporting can go on for another couple of months."

"Gotcha." Clark pointed up the street. "Looks like Paul's here."

The familiar truck pulled up to the curb in front of the building. The window slid down, and Paul waved at them with a grin.

Clark stepped forward and stuck his hand through the open window. "Hey, Paul. How are you doing?"

"Great, Clark. I hear you're giving Rog a hand with his software." The grin widened.

With a shrug, Clark glanced back at Roger. "Nah, I'll leave that to you."

Heat flushed across Roger's cheeks as he rolled his

eyes. "I should know better than to let you two get within speaking distance of each other."

Clark opened the door for Roger. "Your hardware awaits."

"Ha. Ha. Ha," Roger scowled as he punctuated each word. "I'll see you next week." He climbed into the truck.

Paul wrapped his arms around Roger's torso and kissed his ear. "Say goodbye, Clark." He gave Roger's neck a little nibble.

Laughing, Clark slammed the door shut. "Goodbye, Clark." With a wave, he strode down the street.

Roger turned into Paul's embrace and planted a hard kiss on his lover's lips. Paul's arms tightened, squeezing wonderfully as he deepened their kiss.

After lingering a moment, Paul pulled back and patted Roger's leg. "I love you, babe."

Warmth filled Roger as he strapped himself in. He never got tired of hearing Paul's affirmation of his affection. "Love you, too. Thanks for picking me up."

Paul shifted the truck into gear and pulled into traffic. "Since you're off early, would you come with me to my lawyer's office?"

With his eyebrows shooting wide, Roger stared at Paul. "Why?"

"Nothing serious. I'm updating my will, and Anthony convinced me to name someone to make medical decisions should something happen." He stopped at a red light and turned to Roger. "I want you to have power of attorney."

Roger's mouth dropped open. "Are you sure?"

"Hell, yeah, I'm sure." He leaned in and gave Roger

another quick kiss. The light turned green, and Paul continued along Fourth. "Babe, I want you around for a long time. If we split, I still trust you to do right by me if something happens."

"But what about someone in your family?"

Paul's expression became unreadable. "We don't speak. They don't need or want to make decisions about my well-being."

Roger detected the pain in his partner's eyes and shook his head. His own parents were annoying sometimes, but they were always in his corner. They hadn't batted an eyelash when he came out, and he couldn't imagine his life without his parents and their support.

"My attorney and his assistant are awesome people. Jessica is an absolute doll." He chuckled. "She keeps Anthony in line."

"Anthony?"

"The lawyer." His smile turned sad for a brief moment. "We have a shared acquaintance who helped us out."

"Shared?" Roger's curiosity piqued. "In what way?"

"I'll tell you someday." Paul's face returned to the stoic, unreadable expression from before.

Curiosity burned, but he didn't pursue the line of discussion. He stared out the window instead. Back to evasions and refusals to disclose details of his past. Still, he'd managed to get new details. Whatever had happened was bad enough to sever ties between Paul and his parents.

They turned onto Madison, and Paul drove into a parking garage under an older office tower. He pulled into one of the larger parking spots and turned off the engine.

Eyeing Roger, Paul placed his hand on Roger's thigh. "What do you think?"

"Of course, I'll do it for you. Maybe your lawyer should draw up papers for me, too." Roger covered Paul's hand with his own, enjoying the pressure and warmth on his leg. "Right now, my parents would make decisions for me, but I'm sure my mother would be *thrilled* if I changed it to you."

Paul chuckled. "I'm sure." With a final squeeze, Paul pulled his hand away and opened the door. "Let's go."

Roger got out of the truck and pushed the door shut. After locking the vehicle, they strode across the garage to the elevator and pressed the UP button. Paul took Roger's hand, and they held onto each other as they stepped into the carriage and rode up to the seventh floor. Once there, Paul led the way to a single office door with *Anthony Swifson, Attorney at Law* stenciled in block letters across the glass. Paul pressed the buzzer on the doorframe, and a chime sounded inside the office.

A few moments later, a dark-haired man in his mid-thirties answered the door. "Ah, Paul. Nice to see you." He eyed their still clasped hands and broke out into a grin. "And this must be Roger. Paul's gushed about how amazing you are. I'm Anthony Swifson."

"Gushed?" With a chuckle at Paul's darkening cheeks, Roger released his hand from Paul's and shook Anthony's. "Nice to meet you."

Anthony held the door for his clients. "Please, come on in. Jessica waited for you so she could notarize the documents." He led them into a small conference room where a middle-aged woman stood next to the table.

She smiled broadly at their entrance. "Nice to see you again, Paul. Who's this?"

Laying his hands on Roger's shoulders, Paul returned her smile. "Jessica, meet Roger Matthews. He's my partner."

"This is the guy who's won your heart, eh?" She eyed Roger appraisingly. "Quite a catch, Paul. Nice to see you happy and smiling." Stepping forward, she shook Roger's hand. "Definitely a pleasure to finally meet you."

Warmth filled Roger's cheeks. "Thanks."

Anthony rounded the table and sat at the chair across from them. "Shall we get started?"

"Sounds good," Paul said as he pulled out a chair for Roger. After Roger sat, Paul took the seat next to him and set a hand on Roger's thigh.

Passing a pen across to Paul, Anthony nodded at the pile of papers. "The first is the will. I made the changes you requested and everything should be in order."

Paul scrutinized the first page. "So, the sale of my condo goes into trust for any nieces or nephews I might have?"

Nodding, Anthony clasped his fingers in front of him. "Yes, and I've added in the charities you wanted money going to. No mention of your parents or your sister."

Roger's ears perked up. Paul had never mentioned a sister.

Paul took a few minutes to read through the will. "This looks good." He signed the document. "Rog, will you be the witness?"

"Uh, sure." Roger took the pen from Paul and signed.

Jessica applied her notary stamp and filled in the appropriate information, finishing with her signature.

Lifting the completed will from the table, Anthony pushed across the next stack of papers. "Now for the medical directives and the power of attorney. This makes Roger responsible for all medical decisions should you become incapacitated."

"It stipulates no heroic measures to prolong my life, right?" Paul turned to Roger and held him in a steady stare. "You gonna be okay telling the doctors to pull the plug on my life support?"

"No." Roger's eyes widened. "I'm not sure I could ever do that." The sight of Paul laying in a hospital bed plugged into medical equipment as a vegetable flashed into his mind. He closed his eyes and gave a little shake of his head to dispel the image.

Paul set the pen down on the table and took Roger's hand. "I'm not saying at the first sign of trouble cut me off. Only if I'm suffering." He placed kisses along the knuckles of Roger's hand. "I trust you to make the right decision."

Not sure what to say, Roger glanced down at the page. His name adorned the document in bold block letters.

"Besides," Paul said as he tilted up Roger's chin to stare into his eyes. "This is totally hypothetical. Nothing's gonna happen to me."

"This is mostly to protect Paul from anyone else making decisions that he wouldn't want," Anthony chimed in.

"My clients who actually have to invoke these are usually quite elderly."

Roger wasn't sure that made him feel better. His partner was in a dangerous line of work, and anything could happen while he was out on his beat or responding to a call. But Paul trusted him above anyone, a true honor from a man who didn't make friends easily and trusted people even less easily.

Picking up the pen, Roger flipped the page and signed on the line above his name.

Paul wrapped his arms around Roger as Jessica signed and sealed the document. "Thank you, babe."

The warmth and safety of the embrace reassured Roger. "I guess I'd better do one of these as well." He didn't like to think about his mortality, but if he wanted things to progress further with Paul, he should return the trust his lover placed in him.

Releasing him from his hold, Paul nodded. "A good idea. I'm sure Anthony could draw up the paperwork for you."

"Sure," the attorney said as he gathered the documents and handed them to his assistant. "Jessica, would you make copies for Paul?"

"Absolutely." She took the sheaf of papers from her boss and strode around the corner of an internal wall.

"How's your wife doing?" Paul leveled a concerned gaze at Anthony. "Last I heard, she had some medical issues."

Anthony nodded. "Actually, Claire's now my ex-wife. We think the cancer has come back, but she's flying to

California in a couple weeks to visit her sister and have some extensive tests done to determine just what's going on."

Shifting in his chair uncomfortably, Roger glanced at Paul before addressing Anthony. "I'm sorry about your marriage and about your wife."

Anthony gave him a small smile. "I appreciate that, Roger. She decided to divorce me even though I wanted to stay married so she could use the firm's insurance." He hesitated, looking at both of them in turn with a worried frown. Shaking his head, he took a breath. "She figured out I'm gay and told me to stop pretending. She wasn't angry." He drew a steady breath. "I think she was setting things right."

Roger's eyes sprang wide. "Wow, she sounds amazing."

With a nod, Anthony tightened his jaw. "She is."

"How's your son taking it?" Paul wrapped an arm around Roger's waist.

A sad smile stretched across his face. "He's a trooper. We haven't told him about the cancer yet. Better to let him have fun with his cousins in California before the realities of life come crashing down on him." Anthony sighed. "I couldn't ask for a better best friend, though. Claire said she'd stay with me to help with Grayson, but volunteered to move into the guest room in case I want to date. I took the guest room."

Roger sat back in the chair, Paul's arm squeezing him in a protective grip. "She's fine with you dating while she's still living in the house?"

"Apparently, though I'm loathe to do something like that to her." Anthony shook his head. "But I shouldn't be bothering you both with my family weirdness. The only important facts are that Claire's cancer seems to be back, and I'm trying to keep life normal for Grayson. That's about as good as it gets right now."

Jessica returned to the small conference room and handed Paul the papers. "Here you go, Paul. It was lovely to see you."

Grinning at her, Paul pulled his arm away from Roger as he accepted the documents. "You, too, Jessica. Good to see you're keeping this guy in line." He jerked his head toward Anthony.

A bemused grin spread across her lips. "He can be a challenge." She turned to her boss. "I need to get home to Carl. Paul's documents are in the safe, and scanned copies should be in your e-mail to put on the server."

Anthony nodded. "Thanks, Jessica. Have a great night."

She gave the three of them a quick wave and left the conference room.

With a heavy sigh, Anthony sat in the chair across from them. "I don't know what I'd do without Jessica. She's been very helpful with Claire's medical difficulties."

"She's a keeper," Paul agreed. "Congrats on coming out. You seemed miserable, and, frankly, I hoped you'd figure it out."

Anthony shook his head. "Strangely enough, I didn't really put the pieces together until she confronted me. There was the thing with Alex, but that was…" his eyes flicked to Roger for a moment, then back to Paul, "…situational." Another sigh escaped his lips. "I wish I could have just kept on with the charade, but like I said, she wants to be by my side while not getting in the way if I find someone else."

"I found Roger. He's the most amazing thing to happen to me." Paul laid a love-filled gaze on Roger.

Heat surged through Roger as he met Paul's gaze. "I feel the same way."

"Well, Claire is my first priority, and Gray is my second. Nothing else right now matters like those two." Anthony straightened in his chair. "Which leads me to another issue."

Paul cocked his head to the side. "Yes?"

"I think we have a stalker."

Furrowing his brow, Paul leaned forward in his chair. "A stalker? Are you and Claire in danger?"

Anthony shook his head. "No, I think he just wants to rob the place. What do you suggest to keep him at bay?"

"A security system. Maybe cameras and an alarm on the property." Paul kept his gaze firmly on Anthony. "I can come out and patrol the grounds. Maybe a few evenings this week. A police presence might deter your stalker."

Roger tried to keep from huffing. Though great that Paul was so loyal to his attorney, those late night patrols would cut into their already precious time together. Not that Roger could complain too much. His work had kept them apart a large chunk of the last six months. The new assistant at the office couldn't get hired fast enough for him.

With a dismissive wave, Anthony stood. "No, no. I wouldn't want you to do that. I'll get the security cameras installed in the next couple days, but thank you for offering." He checked the expensive watch adorning his wrist. "I'd better get home. Claire will be wondering where I'm at, and we need to get a few of her trip arrangements done this evening."

Roger and Paul stood as well.

Shaking the attorney's hand then patting his shoulder, Paul held him in a firm gaze. "If anything happens, call me. I'll be out there with the county sheriff."

"Thanks, Paul. I appreciate that." He turned to Roger, holding out his hand. "Great to meet you. Let me know if you want me to draw up some documents for you."

"Sure," Roger shook the offered hand. "I'll be in touch."

Anthony walked them to the door and bade them good night. As they waited for the elevator, Roger turned to the man he loved. "He's got a difficult road ahead."

Paul nodded. "Yeah. His kid is adorable. Little Grayson has a lot of personality."

"You're a lot more friendly with Anthony than I'd have expected." Roger clasped his hand, fingers intertwining.

With a squeeze of his hand, Paul chuckled. "Don't be jealous. We have a friend in common, and he's helped with some family issues."

Roger cocked his head to the right. "Your parents and sister?" The surprise on his face must have been evident as

Paul nodded gravely. In the year and a half they'd been together, Paul never spoke about his family except to say they didn't speak. The pain etched in his face every time Roger had brought up the subject of his family was evident at this moment as well.

"What we did here today finishes any contact I'd need to have with them. Thanks for signing. It gives me piece of mind knowing you're the one who'll take care of me." His face brightened. "So, now I want to take you somewhere and spoil you."

Roger laughed. "Spoil me?"

The elevator dinged, and the doors slid open.

With a wriggle of his eyebrows. Paul pulled Roger to the waiting truck. "Definitely."

CHAPTER THREE

"THAT STEAK WAS amazing." Roger slid out of the truck and touched his feet to the cement floor of the condo building's parking garage.

After slamming the door, Paul joined Roger and enfolded him in his strong embrace. He placed light kisses that sent ripples of pleasure along Roger's skin. "I could take you right here," he said, his voice a deep rumble.

Heat coursed through Roger's body, and his cock responded with a twitch in his slacks. "Yes. You could."

Paul released him from his arms and pressed Roger's back against the truck. Eyes full of desire, Paul held Roger's gaze as he sank to the ground and onto his knees. He kissed the tented-out slacks, wrapping his lips around the head of Roger's dick and pressing hard against the fabric of his work pants.

Pushing his back against the cool metal of the truck, Roger widened his stance and reached for the buckle of his belt.

Paul caught his wrists and pushed them behind his back. "Hands off. That's mine." A playful grin spread across his lips. "Behave, or I'll have to cuff you." He returned his lips to the crotch of Roger's slacks, pressing kisses along the stiffened shaft.

With his moans echoing through the garage, Roger sucked in a breath when Paul tugged down the zipper of his fly and reached a beefy hand inside. His fingers caressed the briefs-covered balls and made Roger's cock jolt.

A mischievous grin formed on Paul's face as he reached the waistband of the underwear and tucked the elastic under the hard dick. He eased the shaft though the opening of Roger's slacks and swirled his tongue around the head.

Roger fought to keep his hands off his belt. He wanted to drop his trousers and briefs to give Paul all the access he wanted to his body.

Clearly, though, his lover had other plans. Paul bobbed his head on Roger's shaft, building a delicious pressure in his balls as Paul's hands tugged his dress shirt from his waistband. Flicking each button free with one hand, Paul ran the other along the treasure trail on Roger's abs. Once all the buttons were released and the shirt hung open, he lightly pinched his index finger and thumb around first one then the other of Roger's nipples, applying light pressure.

"Oh, fuck, baby." The jolts of pleasure with each gentle twist flew straight to his cock, making the shaft thicken inside the exquisite embrace of Paul's lips. "You're going to make me come."

Paul's only response was to apply more pressure to his nipples and quicken his pace. Squirming against the truck, Roger's head fell back and bumped against the glass of the passenger window while the pressure in his balls turned into intense tingling.

"You okay?" Paul paused in his sucking to look up at Roger.

"Fuck, yeah," Roger groaned, his cock pulsing. "Don't stop."

The wicked grin returned, and Paul pressed his lips against the leaking head but didn't go further.

Roger tried to nudge his cock farther into Paul's mouth, but Paul kept his lips sealed. "I'll grab my dick and jack off in your face if you don't finish what you started. You're killing me here."

"Don't make any sudden moves. I'm serious about cuffing you." Paul smirked and let his tongue swirl around the head.

"Please, sweetheart," Roger whined, the pressure in his balls rapidly approaching unbearable. "Let me shoot."

Paul gave each nipple another twist, and Roger arched his back with a shout as Paul took his entire cock to the root. Shot after shot blew down Paul's throat as Roger thrashed against the side of the truck, and his screams echoed around the cement walls.

When the orgasm finally subsided, Paul pulled off his cock. "A tasty treat," he said and licked his lips.

Roger struggled to catch his breath as he rested his head against the window. His legs threatened to give way, and his body stiffened when Paul swiped at his cockhead with his tongue. "Fuck!"

Paul chuckled. "I missed a spot." He rose to his feet and pulled Roger into an embrace. "Can you make it upstairs? I could carry you."

With a sigh, Roger melted into Paul's muscular arms. "Carry me."

"You asked for it." Before Roger realized what *carry me* meant, Paul hoisted him over his shoulder and made for the door to the elevator lobby.

Laughing, Roger squirmed. "I thought you'd cradle me in your arms."

With a swat on Roger's butt, Paul echoed his laugh. "I'm saving you the embarrassment of someone coming in the elevator and seeing you with your shirt unbuttoned and your dick hanging out."

The elevator doors opened, and Paul stepped inside, Roger still slung over his shoulder.

Wrapping his arms around Paul's waist, Roger held on as they ascended to the fifth floor. "If you put me down, I'll let you fuck me tonight."

Paul chuckled again. "Is that an either-or proposition?"

Roger grinned. "No, but I thought I'd try it. You can fuck me either way."

The doors slid open, and Paul carried Roger to their condo door. "Reach into my pocket and hand me the key."

Slipping his hand into Paul's jeans, Roger took his time rooting around. He ignored the keys and moved his hand to cup his lover's hardening cock.

With a grunt, Paul chuckled. "That's not my keys."

"Isn't it?" Roger brushed his fingers along the thickening shaft, eliciting a stifled moan from his partner. "Feels like something that ought to be shoved inside a tight opening." He pushed the fabric of the pocket to graze his fingers over the head, feeling a little jerk as Paul's footing faltered.

"Shit, Rog. If you don't stop that and hand me the keys, I'm going to press you up against the wall and take you right here and now."

Roger gave the head another squeeze. "Not seeing the downside here."

Paul hoisted him from his shoulder and set him on his feet. He pinned Roger's hands over his head and claimed his lips. Reveling in the passionate lip-lock, Roger squirmed against the unyielding pressure of Paul's grip holding his hands over his head.

As he broke the kiss, Paul nibbled at the stubble on Roger's chin before sliding his tongue along the sensitive skin of Roger's neck.

Roger moaned at the tingles spreading in the wake of Paul's lips.

Resting his cheek against Roger's, Paul gently bit Roger's earlobe. "You drive me crazy." He licked the space behind Roger's ear.

Barely able to move from the sensations, Roger let out another choked moan and closed his eyes. "It's nothing to what you do to me." His legs would have given way by now if Paul hadn't been holding onto his wrists.

"Seriously, babe. Let's take this to the bedroom. I want you so bad."

The jangle of keys and the releasing of his wrists made Roger open his eyes.

Paul fumbled with the keys, impatient to get inside.

Roger quickly surveyed himself, noticing his achingly hard erection again poking from the front of his slacks and his shirt completely open.

After managing to get the door open, Paul tossed his keys through the doorway and grabbed Roger's arm, pulling him inside the condo, pausing only to kick the door shut, and not stopping until they'd reached the bedroom. He led Roger to the bed and pushed him back. Roger landed on his butt in the middle of the mattress while Paul ripped off his jeans and shirt. His lover stood before him, eyes burning with unconcealed lust as he stepped out of his briefs. His monstrously thick cock jutted in front of him, ready for action.

Roger's heart beat fast as he quickly pulled open his belt and unbuttoned his slacks. Stepping forward, Paul tugged off Roger's shoes then grabbed the legs of his pants and pulled them off in a single yank. He sprang onto the bed, pinning Roger beneath him, and pushed his dress shirt apart and over his arms until his wrists were again held, this time by the fabric and the buttons at the cuffs of his shirt.

"Oh, fuck, Paul. Take me," Roger snarled, animalistic desire pushing rational thought from his mind as he raked his gaze over the muscled cop holding him down.

Paul pressed his hardness between Roger's legs, nudging them apart with his knees. Roger crossed his ankles behind his lover's back and pressed his heels into the firm cheeks of Paul's ass, urging him forward.

Covering Roger's mouth in a flurry of kisses, Paul clawed at the shirt bunched around Roger's wrists. The buttons popped, and the shirt came away, releasing Roger to wrap his hands around Paul's back. Their cocks rubbed together, and Roger squirmed as the prickles of imminent release began.

Surprised by how quickly he was ready to shoot again, Roger groaned. "Sweetheart, you'd better fuck me now. I'm gonna blow again."

Paul kept their dicks grinding together, but pushed up onto his hands and stared down at Roger. "Babe, I want to ask you something."

His eyes wide, Roger clawed the sheets in frustration as Paul gyrated his hips and intensified the tingles through his balls. "Now?" he choked out.

"Yeah." With a wicked grin, he thrust forward.

With bunches of sheet clutched tightly in his hands, Roger fought to keep from falling over the edge into orgasm. "Oh, fuck. Ask me later."

Paul chuckled. "It's relevant to our current situation."

Taking a deep breath, Roger tried to quell his frustration at the delay. "What?"

Paul's dark brows furrowed. "Have you been with anyone else since we got serious?"

Roger blinked and pushed up on his elbows. "Of course not. You're the only man I want."

A smile lit his face. "I haven't either. You're everything I need." He bit his lip before continuing. "We always use condoms, but all my tests are clear."

"Mine, too." Roger cocked his head to the side. "Do you want me bare?"

With a nod, a renewed hunger in Paul's eyes pleaded

with Roger. "Desperately." Paul cupped his hand to Roger's cheek and caressed a thumb across his cheek.

Leaning forward, Roger pressed their lips together while he slid a hand through Paul's short hair to hold him in place. Their lips molded together and parted, allowing Roger to swipe his tongue against Paul's. The kiss intensified, and Paul lowered them both, his full weight resting on Roger as their bodies ground together.

After a few long, delicious moments, Paul's lips left Roger's, and he raised his torso while keeping their erections pressed together. "You have to say it, babe."

The ache in Roger's body only intensified at Paul's request. He squirmed under his lover's weight, spreading his legs wide, then pulling them up until Paul's cock lay along the crevice of Roger's ass. "I want you to fuck me bare. Hard. Pounding." He pulled Paul on top of him until their gazes locked and their lips were only inches apart. "And I want you to shoot inside me."

Paul's dick pulsed between them as they pressed their lips together again. Reaching across the bed to the nightstand, Paul continued to kiss Roger as he fumbled for the drawer holding the lube. He broke their kiss and pushed up. Popping the top of the bottle, he drizzled a heavy dollop against Roger's hole.

The cool of the lube made Roger gasp, and Paul chuckled as he closed the bottle. "Sorry." After tossing the bottle back into the open drawer, Paul spread the lube around Roger's pucker and dipped a finger inside.

A moan escaped Roger's lips at the luscious pressure, and he pushed his body to take more of the wriggling digit. A second finger spread him further and pressed against the hard button of his prostate. Jolts of pleasure fired through his body with each nudge and caress.

Impatient at the incredible sensations swirling inside him, Roger pulled his knees to his chest. "Take me, Paul. I'm ready."

Withdrawing his fingers, Paul slicked his cock and pressed the head at Roger's entrance. Slowly, but with a steady pressure, the thick shaft pushed its way inside, the silkiness of Paul's hardness sliding easily deeper.

Roger rolled back his eyes, closing his lids and savoring the fullness of his lover's cock inside him.

"God, Rog, you feel incredible." Paul paused as the full length of his dick rested inside Roger. "Doing okay, babe?"

Roger's voice strained from the pleasure cascading through his body. "Take me," he rasped as he rocked his hips and squeezed the muscles of his ass around the thickness filling him.

A moan forced its way out of Paul's mouth, and his torso stiffened. "Keep doing that, and I won't last."

"Then you'd better start fucking me." Roger squeezed his ass again.

Paul grunted. Pulling almost entirely out, he angled his thrusts to pound against Roger's prostate.

Roger cried out, the fierce tingling in his balls returning with a vengeance and warning of his impending orgasm. Each prod against his button made his dick harden between them and the intensity of the tingling increase. He squeezed as Paul thrust in, and his lover's rhythm faltered.

"Fuck, Rog, I'm gonna come."

The thrust pounded against Roger's prostate and made his cock jump. After one more direct hit, Roger flew over the edge, squeezing his ass and painting their stomachs with his load.

Paul threw back his head and buried his cock deep, roaring out his release.

Warmth spread inside Roger as his partner filled him. He slipped his legs around Paul as the panting man fell forward, pressing his lips into Roger's neck in a series of feathery kisses.

Wrapping his arms around Paul, Roger held him tight, still trying to recover from his own release. "Amazing."

With a nod, Paul nuzzled against his shoulder. "I love you."

Roger squeezed his arms tighter around Paul. "I love you, too." He rolled them onto their sides, and Paul carefully withdrew his softening cock.

Laying with his arm beneath Roger, Paul used the other hand to caress his fingers along Roger's cheek. "You made a mess. I'll get us a warm rag."

With an arch of an eyebrow, Roger caught Paul's wrist. "Me? You're the one who made love to me so perfectly I couldn't hold back."

Paul chuckled and pulled down his wrist so their fingers intertwined. He brought Roger's knuckles to his lips and slowly kissed each one. "I'm glad you moved in, Rog. It feels so right that you live with me. Glad you don't have to run back to your apartment for a change of clothes before work."

"It means I'm with you all the time now." Roger stared into his dark brown eyes, the implications of their living together still troubling him. "Are you sure you're going to be able to put up with me?" Fear that Paul wouldn't be able to handle such close proximity long-term bubbled into his mind.

"Not a problem." Paul leaned forward and kissed him. "I only need one thing from you. Or at least to consider."

The way Paul's glance locked with his told Roger this was important. "What's that?"

"Give Jason another chance."

Roger sighed. "We'll see." The thought of even seeing Jason Lynch again brought a flurry of anger to an otherwise perfect moment. "Let's get cleaned up."

"Hey, I'm serious." Paul kissed his hand again then untwined their fingers. "He was a total dick, and I get you're angry. But if this is gonna work, I need you boys to make peace and get along."

"I'll think about it." Roger ran his hand over his stomach and lifted a finger. "Now, go get that washcloth, or I'll wipe this mess all over your face."

Holding up his hands in surrender, Paul laughed. "Okay, okay." He rolled off the bed and stood. "But when you're ready, I'll be happy to arrange a meeting."

Roger scooted to the edge of the bed and sat, swiping his sticky fingers at Paul. Dodging, Paul hurried toward the bathroom. His legs a little shaky, Roger reached out his non-gooey hand to steady himself against the wall and stood. He paused a moment, considering Paul's request.

Yeah, he'd eventually have to figure out how to calmly discuss what had happened with Jason, but right now he was still too furious.

CHAPTER FOUR

T HE ALARM SOUNDED through the bedroom, jarring Roger awake. He reached out and swiped at his phone to shut off the klaxon then rolled to his side to discover he was alone in the bed. The sound of the shower running caught his attention, and he pushed his tired body up and out of the warmth of the sheets.

With a groan, he stood, preferring to stay in bed but knowing he needed to get to work early to prepare for the afternoon progress report to Herrington, Angelica, and Marsha. He padded across the hardwood floor to the bathroom, pulling open the door to a cloud of steam. Paul stood in the shower as Roger pulled open the stall door, dark skin covered in white suds from the bar of soap he was rubbing across his broad chest.

A devilish grin slid across Paul's face as he held out the soap and dropped it to the floor. The bar splashed in the sudsy water and bounced into the corner of the stall. "Oops." Turning away, he bent over, pushing his firm, round butt out toward Roger.

Eyeing the inviting spread of his lover's ass, Roger traced a finger along the trail of short hairs lining the crevice. He paused at the pucker, but instead of dipping inside, he lifted his hand and gave Paul's cheek a firm smack.

Paul shot up and turned. "Ouch!" he laughed. "What was that for?"

"For tempting me when I have to get to work. Move over." Roger stepped into the shower and clicked the door shut. He turned into the spray and rinsed off his face.

Strong arms wrapped around him, and a stiff rod pressed against his ass. Paul kissed along his shoulder to his neck and lightly nipped at the skin. "You're so beautiful."

Roger closed his eyes as he leaned back against Paul's firm chest and savored the strong embrace.

"I love the sapphire of your eyes. The wavy locks of your hair. Your lean muscles and perfect body." He trailed his lips to Roger's ear, pressing kisses behind the outer shell and gently grasping the lobe between his teeth. "I love your intelligence. Your kindness. You make me feel special."

"You are special," Roger gasped. His cock stirred at the delicious cadence and seductive tone of his partner's voice.

Paul loosened his embrace to run a hand down Roger's chest. "I love you more than anyone or anything, Roger Daniel Matthews." He spoke each of Roger's names slowly, voice dripping with seduction and raw need. "And I want you."

With a ragged breath and a raging erection, Roger slowly rotated in Paul's grip and surrendered to a tender, gentle kiss. The warm water cascaded over his back while Paul crushed their bodies together and intensified their connection.

Gasping for air, Roger pulled back. "Fill me again. Mark me as yours like you did last night." He stepped back from Paul's arms, turned, and pressed his hands against the wall.

Paul wasted no time, placing his cock at Roger's pucker and pressing forward. Some of the lube from the prior evening's sex remained, and Paul slid in easily, though his entry was accompanied by a slight sting. Roger breathed though the sensation of being filled, surrendering his body to his lover. When he was completely buried, Paul wrapped a strong arm around Roger.

As he bucked back, Roger moaned, "Take me hard."

With a forward thrust, Paul set a forceful rhythm, pounding Roger as he held him firmly in place. The steam from the shower added to the haze of his lust as he took everything his lover gave him, his own cock bouncing with each inward stroke. Their lovemaking the night before, Paul's words filled with love, and the feeling of him sealing their union without a condom, all primed Roger for another explosion.

Increasing the tightness of his hold, Paul pounded harder. "I'm gonna come."

"Do it," Roger cried out, wrapping one hand around his cock and stroking furiously.

With a roar, Paul rammed deep. "Roger!"

Warmth flooded inside Roger as he brought himself to the brink of orgasm. Paul pulled back and thrust forward again, sending a final jolt across his prostate and shoving him screaming over the edge.

They stood under the spray, panting and trying to

catch their breaths. Paul didn't let go. He rested his head on Roger's shoulder as they sucked in the steamy air. After a few moments, Paul's cock slipped out, and he sighed as he straightened.

Roger placed his forehead against the shower wall. "Holy fuck, that was incredible."

Still breathing hard, Paul ran the bar of soap over Roger's back. "I meant every word."

With a push off of the wall, Roger turned to face Paul and raised a hand to his cheek. "I love you so much."

After a quick kiss, Paul washed him, paying special attention to his cock and balls. Once they were finished with the shower, Paul stepped from the stall and handed him a towel. Roger dried off, noticing his pruned hands. He chuckled at the sight.

Paul arched an eyebrow. "What?"

"Good thing the condo has a tankless water heater." He raised his hand to show Paul his fingers. "For how long we were in there, a traditional tank wouldn't have had enough water for us to finish and clean up."

Paul shrugged. "If it had gotten cold, I'd have just shut off the shower and kept going. Want a ride in to work?"

"Sure," Roger grinned. "That means more time with you. Are you working late tonight?"

"Nope. Just a quiet evening at home getting nailed by the man I love." He gave Roger a sweet smile. "It's your turn to fill me."

"If I didn't have a presentation today, I'd say we should call off work and spend the day in bed." Tempting as that thought was, he knew Herrington wouldn't be too happy to have the project delayed, and Marsha would flip her shit.

"Good things come in those who wait."

Roger cocked his head to the side. "Isn't that good things come *to* those who wait?"

The smile turned lecherous. "Not in this case."

Laughing, Roger snapped Paul with the towel. "Let's get dressed before we both get in trouble with our bosses."

They strode into the bedroom, and Roger glanced at the clock. He hurried to the closet and pulled out his dress shirt. "Shit, I wanted to leave half an hour ago."

"Don't stress, babe," Paul said as he pulled on a polo shirt. "You'd be late if you were catching the bus. I'll get you to work on time."

They finished dressing in silence, and Paul left the room while Roger knotted the red tie he reserved for presentations he wanted to shine at. Staring into the mirror, he made sure he looked completely dressed for success then slipped on the suit jacket and hurried from the room.

When he got to the kitchen, he heard the whirr of the juicer. Rounding the corner, Paul lifted the pitcher from the base of the machine and poured two glasses of green juice. He handed one to Roger, and they clinked their glasses together.

Roger stared at the liquid. "What's this?"

"Spinach, cucumber, ginger, apple, and kiwi. Drink up." Paul took a swig and then nodded toward Roger's glass as he swallowed.

Taking a sip of the concoction, Roger was pleasantly

surprised at the fresh taste of the drink. He finished it in three gulps and set the glass in the sink.

Paul chuckled as he rinsed his glass. "Guess you liked it."

"Definitely. Ready to go?"

With a nod, Paul led the way to the front door and held it open. "After you."

They stepped out into the cold parking garage, and Paul again held open the truck door for Roger.

The drive into downtown went surprisingly quickly, and Roger always marveled at how well Paul knew the streets, actively avoiding the worst traffic congestion by taking side routes Roger would never have thought of.

They pulled up to Roger's building, and Paul flipped on his hazard lights in the load zone. Turning, Paul placed a firm hand on Roger's thigh. "See you tonight, babe. I'm taking you somewhere special for dinner. You look amazing."

Leaning forward, Paul molded his lips to Roger's. He tasted of the fresh flavor of the juice Paul had made for breakfast, and Roger lingered in the kiss.

Reluctantly, he knew he had to get inside, so he broke away from his lover. "I can't wait. Be careful out there."

Paul winked with a grin. "I always am."

AT THREE O'CLOCK, ROGER'S cell buzzed in his pocket as he stood next to the door about to go meet with Herrington before the presentation to the partners. He fished for his cell and glanced at the screen. Though the full number was unfamiliar, he recognized the prefix as a City of Seattle number. He pressed ACCEPT and held the phone to his ear.

"Hello?"

"Roger, it's Jason Lynch." His voice sounded strained.

A flush of irritation washed over Roger as he rolled his eyes. "I'm surprised to hear from you," he snapped. "I wouldn't think you'd want to speak to a *freeloader* like me."

"Shit. Roger, uh…"

He frowned as a worry niggled at the back of his mind. "Is there something wrong?" Jason Lynch wouldn't be calling him from his work phone, especially after what happened, if there wasn't something major going on. And why wasn't it Paul calling?

"Do you have a medical directive for Paul?"

All the heat drained from his face as he reached out for the wall to steady himself. "It's at the condo. Why?"

"Can you get it and bring it up to Harborview?"

"What's happened?" Roger pressed his back to the wall and slid to the floor.

A heavy sigh sounded through the phone. "We were responding to a domestic violence call out in Skyway. When we got there, the husband had the wife outside, threatening her with a gun. As we got out of the car, the guy trained the gun on Paul and got two rounds off before I took him down."

A chill gripped Roger as the panic rose in his voice. "Is Paul dead?"

"No, but he's in bad shape. How fast can you get

here?"

His hand shook as he struggled to keep the phone next to his ear and his emotions in check. "Uh, I don't have my car. Paul brought me in and was going to pick me up after work."

Herrington strode into his office at that moment. "Are you ready to…" He broke off, his eyes widening as he stared down at Roger. Concern flashed across his face. "Roger?"

"Hold on, Lynch." Roger looked up into his boss's face. "Paul's been shot." His lip trembled as he fought the tears threatening to burst forth.

Kneeling down, Herrington placed a strong hand on Roger's shoulder. "How can I help?"

He took in a ragged breath. "I need to get the medical directive from our condo and get up to Harborview."

Herrington nodded in his usual take-charge manner. "You're in no shape to drive. Finish your call and get your coat. I'll meet you out front in five minutes."

A wave of emotion threatened to tear down the dam of shock holding back his impending breakdown. He fought hard to keep control. "Thanks."

Herrington pushed upward and strode from the office.

"Roger, are you still there?" Jason's voice brought him back to the phone call.

"Um, my boss is going to bring me." He focused his mind on remembering where Paul had placed the large manila envelope from Anthony Swifson.

"Okay. He's in surgery right now. I'll leave instructions with the receptionist to get you into the ICU. If you have a power of attorney, bring that, too."

A tremor shook his body. "It'll probably be an hour before I can get there."

"That's okay. He'll still be in surgery. We need to get the paperwork going so you won't have to be distracted by it once he's in his room." Jason paused. "Look, Roger, I'm sorry about what happened between us, and I want you to know that both Mike and I are here if you need anything at all."

Unsure what to say, Roger pushed himself up the wall on shaky legs. "I'll be there as quickly as I can."

"Okay. See you soon." The phone beeped twice, ending the call.

Roger staggered to his desk, grabbed a half-empty glass, and downed the water. He sat for a moment on his desk and considered whether he should find a way to contact Paul's family. Though Paul had been adamant they wouldn't care about his wellbeing, he felt they should at least be told their son was in the hospital. Roger shook his head. He'd see about calling them after he had something to tell them.

Standing away from his desk, Roger took a deep breath and braced himself for the next few hours. He couldn't lose control. He focused on the documents he needed to retrieve then grabbed his coat from the hook and shut off the light in his office. He hurried to the reception area and found his boss speaking with Elsibeth.

She stood, stepped around the desk, and threw her arms around him. "I'm so sorry. You call me if you need anything at all."

Roger hugged her back. "I will. Thank you."

With a final squeeze, she let him go. "If you get a chance, let me know how he is."

Herrington set his trademark fedora on his head. "Ready to go?"

"Yeah." They strode out the door.

TRUE TO HIS WORD, Jason had informed the front desk that Roger was coming, and the receptionist directed him to the ICU. Herrington had dropped him off and told him to call if he needed a ride later. The orderly at the nurse's station outside the ICU opened the door for him, and he strode down the hall and into the reception area.

Jason stood and met him at the desk. The tall officer hesitated before extending his hand. "Hello, Roger."

Standing in the hospital with his lover in intensive care was no place to hold a grudge. Roger stepped forward and hugged him. "Thanks for calling me."

Patting his back, Jason returned the embrace. "Of course." Breaking the hug, Jason addressed the nurse. "This is Officer Tomlinson's partner, Roger Matthews."

Roger focused on the stern-faced woman. "I have the medical directives and the power of attorney here."

She took the papers from him and scanned them. "Thank you. I'll make copies for his file. It looks like Officer Tomlinson is out of surgery. You should be able to go back shortly. Please have a seat." She stood and walked into the office area behind the desk.

Jason led him to the chairs in the waiting area and sat

next to him. "That bastard hit him in the chest. The doctor said one of the bullets lodged in his lung, and the other severed a major blood vessel. One of the neighbors was an EMT and knew what to do to apply the right pressure until the ambulance got there."

Anger flared in Roger. "What happened to the guy who shot him?"

"He's dead. I hit his arm with the first shot, but he turned, and the second bullet went through his heart." Jason leaned forward and ran his hands down his face. "I didn't intend to kill him."

Roger didn't feel especially sad the bastard was dead, but he wrapped an arm around Jason's back. "You were protecting yourself and your fellow officer. Is the woman okay?"

Jason nodded. "She took a beating, but she'll be okay."

The doors opened, and a short, dark-haired doctor of South East Asian descent stepped into the waiting area. "Officer Lynch?"

Both Jason and Roger stood and approached the surgeon.

She looked at the two men. "I'm Doctor Sakurai."

Jason nodded at Roger. "This is Officer Tomlinson's partner, Roger Matthews."

"The good news is, he's out of surgery. That EMT knew what she was doing and saved him from bleeding out. We were able to repair and re-inflate the lung." She paused. "Unfortunately, the other bullet tore him up pretty badly and grazed his heart."

What warmth had returned to Roger's body quickly

drained away. "What does that mean?"

"We've repaired as much of the damage as we can, but the rest is up to him." She sighed. "I'm sorry it's not better news, but he's alive."

The dryness in his throat made it hard to speak. He glanced at Jason, who seemed equally white-faced as his jaw tightened. Roger returned his attention to the doctor. "Is he going to survive?" The words almost choked him, but he managed to get them out.

With a deepening frown, she sighed. "Like I said, we've taken care of as much of the damage as we could. It's taken a lot out of him, and he did lose quite a bit of blood. The next twenty-four hours will be critical."

"And if he does pull through?" He knew Paul was going to pull through. He had to.

"Depending on his strength, he will likely have a long recovery period. He'll need respiratory therapy as well as physical therapy because of the lung."

Jason set a hand on Roger's shoulder. "Can we see him?" The gesture provided some comfort to the numb-ness consuming Roger.

She nodded. "He's on a respirator and sedated, so he won't be able to speak to you. Follow me."

Leading them through the large double doors, the doctor strode down the white corridors. She paused at a doorway toward the end of the hallway.

Roger stepped inside the room and immediately went still, struggling with the sight that met him. Paul lay on his back, a large tube disappearing into his mouth and IVs taped to the tops of his hands. Two large bandages covered the majority of his chest. His coloring seemed far too light, almost grey, and his eyes were closed. The machine next to his bed beeped rhythmically, accompanied by the sucking sound of the life support machine.

Placing a steadying hand on Roger's back, Jason nudged him forward.

Stepping farther into the room, Roger stood next to Paul's bed. Careful not to disturb the IVs, Roger grasped his lover's hand, pressed his palm to Paul's, and laced their fingers together. "Paul?" His voice quaked.

A scrape along the floor made Roger glance over his shoulder. Jason moved a chair next to the bed. "Why don't you sit down. I'll get you some coffee from the cafeteria, unless you want something else."

"Coffee's great. Thanks." Roger returned his stare to his partner, keeping a grip on his hand as Jason left the room. "I'm here with you." He leaned forward and kissed Paul's cheek.

Paul's hand twitched against his.

"Paul?"

Another twitch, but this time definitely more of a squeeze.

Though Paul didn't open his eyes, Roger took it as a response. "I'm not going anywhere, sweetheart. You'd better stay with me, too."

After one final twitch, Paul's hand relaxed. Roger lifted their hands and pressed his lips against the fingers that had only that morning caressed his face before his lover had dropped him off at work. Though still worried beyond belief, he had hope that Paul would pull through.

Roger couldn't imagine life without the handsome cop who made him complete.

CHAPTER FIVE

"MR. MATTHEWS?" A HAND tapped against his shoulder.

With a start, Roger's eyes flew open as adrenalin coursed through his body. "Yes? What's wrong?"

The orderly shook his head. "No, everything's fine. I'm sorry to wake you, but I need to give Officer Tomlinson a bath and change his dressings."

Drowsiness clouded his thoughts. "Oh, okay. What time is it?"

"It's seven in the morning."

"Oh, shit. I must have fallen asleep." He rose from the chair. "I'll be in the waiting area. Can you come get me when you're done?"

The young man smiled as he placed a plastic basin filled with water onto the table next to the bed. "Absolutely."

Roger nodded his thanks and stepped from the darkened room into the bright light of the hallway. He had to shield his eyes for a moment, until they became accustomed to the glare. Fishing his cell from his pocket, he scrolled through the long list of messages. Three missed calls from his boss, two from Jason, five text messages from

Clark, and a call and voicemail from his mother.

He swiped the notification by her name and pressed play on the message.

"Hi, sweetie. Your father saw on the news this evening that an officer had been shot. Is Paul okay? Give me a call when you can. We love you both, honey. Buh-bye."

Seven was a little early to call his mother, though he guessed she was already up and having her second cup of coffee of the morning. His parents had embraced Paul with open arms, and his mother especially had a soft spot for his boyfriend. She'd been pushing them both to move in together. He assumed her goal was to welcome a son-in-law into the family. Both he and Paul had a good chuckle on several occasions at her obvious hints at matrimony.

Refocusing on his priorities, he whipped off a quick text to Clark, asking him to cover for him today. His cell rang a couple of seconds later.

Clark's voice burst through the speaker, the pace of his words frantic. "What happened? I heard on the radio that an SPD officer had been shot, and Herrington told me it was Paul."

"Yes, it was. I'm in the Harborview ICU ward. Paul's on life support, but he's alive." He sighed heavily. "Actually, it's pretty bad."

"Geez, Roger. Do you need anything?" The concern in his voice carried through the cell.

"Could you cover for me a couple days at work?" Roger huffed as he considered his position. "Normally, I'd have the assistant hold down the fort, but since Marsha ran the last four off, I don't have any backup."

"I can take a couple days off here this week. My boss is pretty flexible about the schedule as long as I get my work done. We're in between events at the moment."

A swell of emotion threatened to make Roger break down. "You're the best."

"If you need me to come sit with Paul while you get some sleep or take care of things at work, just let me know. Like I said, I'm flexible."

Pulling himself together, Roger stood and walked toward the men's room. "Jason Lynch has offered to be here with Paul, as well as his partner Mike."

The tone in Clark's voice changed from concerned to protective. "You mean that douche of a beat partner? You shouldn't let him anywhere near Paul after what he said about you."

Roger paused at the doorway of the restroom. "He apologized, and, frankly, holding a grudge while someone we both care about is unconscious in the ICU ward wouldn't help. He's genuinely sorry, and I can accept that."

"You're a better man than me," Clark spat. "I'd have popped him in the nose."

"He had to shoot the guy that got Paul and ended up killing him. I can't imagine that's easy to deal with—no matter what the circumstances." Leaning against the wall next to the door, Roger let loose a long exhale. "He's not a bad guy. Don't be too angry at him."

"Okay, okay. I'll be nice if we cross paths. The offer is always open if you need me there." He paused for a moment. "Hey, I need to get going. Don't worry about

Marsha or the office. I know how to tame the savage marketing beast."

Roger chuckled. "I owe you big-time."

"No, you don't. This is what friendship is all about. Talk to you soon." The phone beeped twice as the call ended.

Ducking into the restroom, Roger hurried into the last stall and shut the door. He shuddered as he let the dam burst on his emotions. Grabbing a wad of toilet paper, he blew his nose as his tears flowed.

After allowing himself some time to melt down, he pressed his back against the tiled wall and blew his nose a final time before tossing the toilet paper into the bowl. He stood and relieved himself, flushed, then left the stall and washed his hands. Looking into the mirror as the warm water ran over his fingers, Roger surveyed his condition. Red-rimmed eyes stared back at him under disheveled hair. He grabbed two paper towels from the dispenser, dried his hands, and wiped his face with the damp paper.

The door opened behind him, and Jason Lynch stepped inside. "Oh, hey, Roger. I thought I'd check in on you and Paul. You doing okay?"

"Yeah, I'm all right. The orderly is giving him a spit bath right now." Roger stepped to the door.

Jason moved to the urinal. "I'll be right out."

After leaving the restroom, Roger returned to the seating area. As he was about to sit, the orderly carried the empty plastic basin from Paul's room. The young man waved, nodded, and headed for the nurse's station.

Roger considered running to the cafeteria for a cup of

coffee, but he decided to return to Paul. The life support machine filled the quiet of the room with a steady rhythm. He approached Paul's bed, looking for signs of improvement. Paul's coloring was definitely better this morning. Some of the grey had darkened to a more normal coloring, and his lips didn't have the bluish tinge he'd seen the prior evening.

A rap at the door caught Roger's attention.

Waving, Jason stood in the doorway. "Hey, mind if I come in?"

"Not at all." Roger took the chair next to the bed.

Jason entered and sat on the upholstered bench against the wall. "How is he this morning?"

"The doctor hasn't been in yet, but I think he looks better." Roger's thoughts returned to the doctor's words. "Do you think we should contact Paul's family in case he doesn't pull through?"

With a frown, Jason crossed his arms. "I don't know, Roger. Is that a good idea? I've never heard Paul mention them other than to say they don't speak."

"He pretty much said the same to me, but I think they'd want to know he's in bad shape." He considered his own mother and father, knowing he needed to call them to break the news. They'd be worried about Paul, especially since Roger hadn't called or texted to say he was okay. "If it were me, my parents would want to know."

"I can see if I can dig up something on them." Jason looked dubious. "This may not be a good idea, but I suppose you're right."

Doctor Sakurai knocked at the doorframe. "Good

morning."

"Hello," Roger said and straightened in the chair.

"I came by to see how Officer Tomlinson's doing." She moved to the keyboard and used the mouse to click through several screens. "His breathing is regular, which is a good sign. If he continues to improve, we'll remove the respirator."

After a quick glance at a worried Jason, Roger addressed the doctor. "Doesn't he need the respirator to take over for the damaged lung?"

"At the moment, he does, but if he continues to gain strength, we'll give his lungs a chance to work on their own." She clicked through a couple more screens, typed some notes, and locked the computer. "The longer he stays on the respirator, the more chance he has of getting pneumonia." She stepped toward the bed. "His coloring is looking better."

Roger nodded. "I was thinking that, too."

"He made it through the night, and that's another good sign." Crossing the room, she paused at the door. "I'll be back later this afternoon. If you need anything, Callie at the nurse's station can help."

"Thanks, doc."

After the doctor left the room, Jason rose. "I might follow her out and get some coffee. Roger, you want something from the cafeteria?"

As if on cue, Roger's stomach rumbled. "If they have some sort of breakfast sandwich, I'd like that." He fished in his pocket for his wallet.

Jason held up his hand. "I got this. Want some coffee?"

Arching an eyebrow, Roger frowned. The shadow of their falling out blazed across his thoughts, fanning a defensive anger. "I can afford it," he snapped.

"I know you can, Roger. I wasn't insinuating anything." Jason echoed his frown. "Let me get this one. You can buy the next round."

"Sorry. Thanks." Roger sat back, feeling foolish. Jason had apologized already, and he kicked himself for being ungracious. "That's kind of you."

"No problem." Jason hesitated. "Look, I understand. You have no reason to take me at my word after my colossal fuck up."

Huffing a breath of air, Roger chuckled. "Don't worry about it. If I didn't trust you, you wouldn't be here. I appreciate you getting me breakfast and helping out."

"So, we're good?" His eyes were wide and hopeful.

"Yeah, Jason. We're good."

"Thanks." He nodded. "I'll be back in fifteen minutes."

"Take your time." Roger's stomach growled again.

Jason laughed. "I won't be long."

"Hey, Mom. It's Roger."

"Good morning, sweetie." Her cheerful voice rang through the cell. "How are you boys doing this morning?"

"Well…" He hesitated, not wanting to ruin her morning.

"Honey, what's wrong?" Her tone changed, reflecting

immediate worry. "Oh, no. It was Paul, wasn't it?"

A little tremor shook him, and he fought back the sob threatening to force its way out. "Yeah."

"Where are you? Do you need me to come?"

Even at thirty-three, Roger felt the urge to fall into his mother's embrace and hope she could protect him from the awful realities of a world where the man he loved had been shot and was stuck in a hospital bed, a machine breathing for him. He didn't want her to see Paul in that state. Didn't want her to worry. "Not yet. If he gets worse, or…" His voice trailed off as he fathomed a life where Paul didn't make it. The numbness from before settled on him again.

His mother's voice brought his focus back. "If you need us, Dad and I can come. You know we're always here for you both."

"Thanks, Mom. Uh," his voice shuddered, and he paused a moment to regain control. "I'll call you when I have some more news."

"We love you, sweetie. Let us know how we can help."

"I will. Love you, too." Roger ended the call and slipped the phone into his pocket. Though he needed to call his boss, he also needed to get himself under control.

Jason returned to the room a few minutes later. "Breakfast is served." He set a plate with a sausage, egg, and Swiss-cheese breakfast sandwich on the stand next to the chair. "They also had bacon, but this looked a little more substantial. Did you have dinner last night?"

Shaking his head, Roger smelled the sandwich, and his stomach rumbled again. "No, I fell asleep, and the nursing staff were as quiet as church mice."

"I'd guess you needed the rest after the shock of yesterday." Jason handed over a cup of coffee. "I need to run into work for a bit. More paperwork to fill out and such. I'll see what I can find on Paul's family."

Roger took a sip of the coffee, grateful for the caffeine hit and the warmth filling his belly. "Thanks. I appreciate you doing that for me."

"No problem." With a quick look at Paul, Jason turned and left the room.

Just as Roger took a bite of the sandwich, the cell in his pocket buzzed. With his mouth full, he tried to quickly chew as he pulled out the phone and checked the display. *W. Herrington* in white block letters overlaid on a picture of his boss's fedora filled the screen.

Swallowing, Roger accepted the call and brought the cell to his ear. "Good morning, Mr. Herrington."

"Hello, Roger. How are things going?" Herrington's gruff voice couldn't hide his concern.

"Paul made it through the night, but he's still on life support. The doctor wants to get him off the machine as soon as possible so he doesn't get pneumonia." Roger's gaze fell to Paul. His lover seemed to sleep peacefully, though Roger knew full well the sedative in the IV drip helped with that.

"Try not to worry. I'm sure he'll pull through just fine." Herrington cleared his throat. "Mr. Adamson informed me that he'll come in a couple days this week to help out."

"I didn't want to leave you all in the lurch. Clark can

handle the day-to-day stuff."

Herrington chuckled. "And he's shown quite a talent for artfully maneuvering around Ms. Fisher."

For the first time in two days, Roger laughed. "Yeah, he's pretty amazing."

"While we, of course, are grateful for his help, we can manage a few days without you. Don't worry about things here. Just concentrate on your exceptional companion and his recovery."

Emotion welled in Roger again. "Thank you, Mr. Herrington. I really appreciate that."

"I'll let you go. Marsha just came into my office. Let me know how things are going." The call ended with two beeps.

Roger returned the cell to his pocket.

With all the calls he needed to make complete, he took Herrington's advice and concentrated on Paul. He ran his fingers along Paul's arm and kissed his forehead. "Stay with me, Paul. Keep fighting."

CHAPTER SIX

J ASON KNOCKED AT the door of Paul's room. "Good afternoon, Roger. How are you doing?"

Stretching out his back, Roger yawned and pushed up from the chair. "I'm a bit sore, but I'll be okay."

Jason pulled a folded piece of paper from his pocket and stepped into the room. "I found his mother. Her name is Tasheeka Tomlinson, and she's an insurance adjuster in Tampa Bay, Florida."

Roger took the paper and opened it to read the information. He blew out a breath that billowed his cheeks. "Do you think I should call her?"

Jason shrugged. "You're probably doing the right thing. She may or may not want to hear about her son. It has been a long time, after all." Jason turned his gaze to Paul. "But he may not want to see her."

Roger grimaced. "I've thought about that. I think if they make an effort, Paul would be open to seeing them." Worry still niggled at his thoughts.

With a shake of his head, Jason turned back to Roger. "As far as I know, he hasn't made any attempt to contact them since they tossed him out. Paul never went into what happened. He only said he was estranged from his parents, and he doubted they'd ever want to be around him again."

"Well, I'll take the responsibility if he gets upset. His mother may not even talk to me, but if there's any possibility they can reconcile, I feel he should have the opportunity." He read over the number and the address. "I really appreciate you finding this for me."

"No problem." Jason stepped to the chair next to Paul's bed. "You want to grab some food or splash some water on your face? I can sit here for a while."

Roger stretched again, reaching his hands over his head and feeling satisfying pops in his back and neck. "That would be great, thanks." He left the room and blinked his eyes in the glare of the harsh light of the hallway.

After stopping off in the restroom to freshen up, he headed down to the cafeteria and bought a burger and a salad. He sat at one of the tables in the large seating area and ate his meal, fretting over what he'd say to Paul's mother. Inspiration didn't come.

After draining the last of his coffee, Roger threw his plate and the bamboo cutlery into the compost bin and then headed back to the elevator. He returned to the ICU and passed the nurse's station, stopping near the door to Paul's room and sighing. Best to get this over with. Turning on his heel, he walked back along the hallway and looked around the waiting room for somewhere to make his call.

Stepping though a doorway marked Quiet Room, Roger drew the paper Jason had given him and his cell from his pocket and closed the door. Though he had no idea what Paul would think of him contacting his estranged family, Roger hoped they would want to hear about their son.

He hesitated, finger hovering over the keypad. Should he do this? Would Paul be angry? The last thing he wanted to do was upset the person he loved most. He shook his head. No, Paul deserved the chance to reunite with at least one parent. It would be up to his mother whether she wanted the opportunity.

With a deep breath, he punched in the number and held the cell to his ear. After two rings, the call connected.

"This is Tasheeka Tomlinson. How can I help you?"

"Uh, hello Mrs. Tomlinson. My name is Roger, and I'm calling about your son, Paul."

The only response was a small gasp and silence.

A feeling of dread settled over him as he pressed on. "He's been injured on the job, and I thought I should call you."

"Who did you say you were?" Tasheeka's voice shook.

"I'm Roger Matthews. Your son and I have been together for about a year and a half."

Suspicion entered her tone. "I haven't heard from him in fifteen years. Why isn't he calling me?"

"He can't. He's in the ICU ward of Harborview Medical Center in Seattle, Washington, unconscious."

"He's what?" Her voice rose several decibels as the sound of something clattering burst through the phone.

Roger frowned. "Are you okay?"

"Never mind about me. What happened to my son?"

"He's a police officer in Seattle. He and his partner responded to a call, and he was shot." Roger's voice choked, and he paused a second to get his emotions back under control.

"Is he dead?" Her now shrill voice sounded on the verge of tears.

"No. He's still unconscious, but he squeezed my hand yesterday."

"Oh, God." She wailed, her sobs coming clearly through the cell.

A pang in his chest pinched. Roger fought not to join her in her tears. "I know he's going to be okay. He's a fighter."

After a moment, she seemed to get herself under control. "If I come, would you let me see him?"

"Of course. Why wouldn't I?"

"Like I said, Paulser hasn't contacted us since his father threw him out." Anger momentarily replaced the sorrow in her voice. "I divorced that bastard after he cost me my son and almost cost me my daughter. I didn't know where to even start looking for him."

"If you and your daughter want to come, you can stay with me. Our condo has an extra bedroom." Roger paused, surprised that the offer rolled out of his mouth before he had a moment to think about it.

"We have a whole entourage, so we'll find a place near the hospital." She sniffled. "Thank you for calling me."

With the feeling he was digging a deeper hole for himself, Roger pressed on. "Do you have a contact number for his father?"

"Oh, *hell* no!"

Her voice boomed through the cell, and he had to

hold it away from his ear.

"That bastard ain't gettin' nowhere *near* my son."

"Uh, okay." Roger fidgeted in the chair. "I should get back to Paul."

Her voice calmed. "I'll be there tomorrow. What's the name of the hospital again?"

"Harborview Medical Center. It's on Ninth and Jefferson, just south of the downtown core."

"Thanks again. We'll be there tomorrow." With a tone full of purpose, she finished the call.

"Bye." Roger's phone beeped twice, and the call ended. He glanced toward Paul's room. "I hope I did the right thing."

ROGER DIDN'T BOTHER going into work the next morning. Clark had Marsha wrapped around his little finger, and all the outstanding invoices had been paid. His friend had even run payroll and dealt with the various tax payments. Herrington was pleased as punch.

Though Paul hadn't woken up, Roger felt his lover's condition was rapidly improving. Dr. Sakurai seemed to think he would open his eyes soon and had removed the life support machine after checking his progress. Paul's breathing had stuttered somewhat, but quickly evened out as his body took over from the machine. The doctor was pleased, and Roger had breathed a big sigh of relief.

Just after lunchtime and a trip to the cafeteria for a quick bite to eat, Roger walked down the hallway with a half-empty cup of coffee in his hand. He paused outside

Paul's room as a commotion down the hall made him turn his head back the direction he'd just come.

A large woman with her black hair in ringlets, a determined round face, and blue eyeshadow contrasting dramatically with her dark skin, pushed her way through the ICU ward doors. Tasheeka Tomlinson, no doubt about it. Roger almost smiled at the woman who was like a tornado. She was clearly letting nothing get between her and her son. Roger's eyes widened as she nearly flew down the hallway, trailed by a beautiful young woman holding a toddler and a younger man he surmised was the woman's husband.

Tasheeka's eyes widened as she approached Roger, a long, blue fingernail pointed at his nose. "Are you the boy who called me?"

Impulsively taking a step back and bumping against the door frame, Roger nodded as he clutched his cup. "Yes, ma'am. I'm Roger."

She pulled him into a huge hug, and he struggled to keep his coffee from spilling. "Thank you." Squeezing him tight, she held onto him for a moment before releasing him. She held him at arm's length, raking an appraising gaze up and down. "Mmm-mmm, my baby has good taste."

Heat exploded across Roger's face. "Oh, uh, thank you." He glanced through the open doorway. "Paul's inside. They took him off of the respirator this morning. He's able to breathe on his own. The doctor says that's a good sign."

Tasheeka linked her arm in his and pulled Roger into

the room. The family accompanying her followed in her wake without a word.

"Paulser, baby." She let go of Roger and approached the bed. Raising her hand, she caressed his face.

Paul took in an audible breath and released it as his eyes fluttered open.

His pulse racing, Roger set the paper cup on the small table and hurried to stand beside Tasheeka.

"Roger?" A weak voice he barely recognized croaked out of Paul.

"I'm here." Carefully taking his hand, Roger lifted it to his lips and kissed his fingers.

Tasheeka took a step back, allowing Roger to move closer to his lover.

He took a ragged breath. "What happened?"

Roger gave him a little smile. "You got shot by some thug abusing his wife. He hit you in your chest and grazed your heart." Roger squeezed his hand. "You scared the hell out of me."

"Is she okay?" His eyes, still somewhat unfocused, sought out Roger's.

"The woman? Yeah, she's okay. Jason shot the man. He didn't make it."

Paul closed his eyes for a moment then opened them again and squinted at the younger woman still holding the child at the foot of his bed. "Melia? Is that you?"

"Hi, Paulser." She came around the other side of the bed. "I'm so glad you're okay."

He grinned weakly. "Who's this with you?"

A brilliant smile lit up her face. "This is your nephew.

Say hello, Pauley."

The little guy squirmed in her arms and gave a shy wave.

Staring between her and her son, Paul's lips spread into a grin as his eyes drooped sleepily. "You named him Paul?"

"After you, of course."

Paul's brow furrowed. "How did you...know I was...here?"

Tasheeka finally found her voice. "Roger called me." She looked on the verge of tears.

With dilated eyes widening, Paul slowly turned his head to the other side to focus on Tasheeka. "Mamma?"

She brought her hand to her mouth. "Baby."

"Never thought...I'd see you...again." Storm clouds blew across his rapidly focusing eyes. "Never thought you'd want to."

Before she could say anything further, Roger turned to the sound of footsteps entering the room. A tall, burly man stepped through the door and stopped, taking in the scene before him. He had sandy hair mixed with grey, sea-green eyes, and a worn face. In his day, he'd probably played football. It only took Roger a moment to place his features.

Tasheeka turned to face the newcomer, stepping forward to stand between him and the other occupants of the room. "What the hell are you doing here?"

The gathering storm on Paul's face was nothing to the hurricane unleashing before them. If looks could kill, this guy would have been burned to a crisp by her fury.

The man furrowed his brow, not backing down from Tasheeka. "I'm here to see my son."

Paul tugged at Roger's hand, and Roger turned away from the train wreck in progress to the wince of pain on his partner's face.

"What have you done?"

CHAPTER SEVEN

TASHEEKA WHIPPED AROUND to glare at Roger. "Did you call him, too?"

Shaking his head, Roger stepped closer to the bed. "I don't even know who he is. The only person I called was you."

She wheeled around to glare at Paul's father. "How did you find him?"

Clearly not expecting to see anyone with his son, let alone his ex-wife, the man crossed his arms. "Some woman from the Seattle Police Department called me and said my son had been shot."

Her eyes narrowed. "And why would you care? You threw him out the door when he was seventeen."

He turned away from her. "A lot has changed since you walked out on me, Tasheeka."

"Hmphf. You don't have my paycheck for a starter." She bobbed her head, attitude dripping off each word.

"I'm not here to argue with you or dredge up the past." He met her glare with one of his own. "I know I fucked up."

Paul's wheeze and groan cut them off. "Get out. Both of you." His hand went limp inside Roger's grip.

Leaning closer, Roger let go of his hand. "Are you okay?"

"So tired." His eyes fluttered closed. "Stay, Rog?"

"I'll be right here." Roger pulled a chair next to the bed and turned to face Paul's family as he sat. "I think it would be best if you all went out to the waiting room. I'll come get you if he wants to see you."

The younger man with Melia cleared his throat. "You heard what he said." Then he herded Paul's family out of the room.

Paul's sister came around the bed to Roger. "He's going to be upset to see our parents. It didn't go well the last time we were all together, and that's my fault. I told him to come out to them, and that it would be okay. Dad beat him and threw him out the front door with nothing."

Roger stared at Paul for a moment as he slept. "I had no idea. He never talked about your parents, other than to say they didn't want him around." He felt like an idiot. What had he been thinking to contact the people who'd hurt him?

With her free hand, Melia grabbed his shoulder. "You took a chance. It'll be the right thing, I promise."

He looked up at her. "Why do you think that?"

"Mamma divorced Dad over what he did to Paulser. We had no idea where to look for him. Seattle's a long way from southern Florida." She moved to the door. "When he wakes up, tell him I missed him."

Roger watched her leave, shaking his head at the stupidity of Paul's family. How could they throw out someone as loving and loyal as Paul?

"Rog?" The raspy voice brought his attention back to the bed.

Turning to Paul, he reached out and twined his fingers with his lover's. "Right here."

"Why'd you…call them?" His eyes drooped, but he struggled to keep them open. Pain dripped off his words, and Roger was sure it wasn't from the gunshot wounds. "They hurt me."

"I didn't know, sweetheart." Roger dropped his gaze. "I guess I thought they should know if you were dying. When I called your mother, I didn't know if you'd make it. The doctor wasn't optimistic." He shuddered as he tried to keep the emotions that had built up over the last few days from spilling over.

"I'm okay. Not leaving you."

"You'd better not." Roger fidgeted as his mind turned to Paul's partner. "About Jason Lynch."

Scrunching his forehead, Paul groaned. "What'd he do now?"

"Nothing bad. He's been great. I should have listened to you and patched things up sooner." He held Paul's sleepy gaze. "Jason was a total ass, but he apologized, and we're okay now. He called me right away when you were being admitted."

Paul nodded. "He felt bad. Talked…in the car. Wanted…to make it up…to you."

"We're good, sweetheart. He's been terrific while you've been in here."

He frowned, his face screwed up in confusion. "How long?"

"Three days. The first one was a nail-biter." He stood, keeping their fingers connected as he leaned over the bed and kissed Paul's cheek. "You were all tubed up. I knew you'd be okay when you squeezed my hand."

Paul's eyes closed again. "Kiss me again."

Roger molded his lips to Paul's, relishing their first real kiss in three days. Not a deep one, but more than a peck. He lifted his head. "How was that?"

"Perfect," Paul breathed as his eyes opened and locked on Roger's. "Want to ask you something."

"Anything." Roger sat on the chair.

"I love you."

Roger chuckled. "I hope that wasn't the question." He kissed Paul's hand. "Because I love you, too. More than anything or anyone."

A sleepy smile spread across Paul's lips. "Here's the question… If you can put up…with my hours…and my cop buddies…" Paul struggled to keep his eyes open but pushed through.

Roger's heart thumped hard in his chest as he hung on each of Paul's words.

"Will…you marry…me?"

His breath caught. "Are you sure that's not the drugs talking?"

With a slight shake of his head, Paul tightened his grip on Roger's hand. "No. Was waiting…for your birthday. Don't want…to waste…time dating." His eyes closed, but he pushed them open again. "If I…don't make it…want you…to know…how I feel."

A searing tear slid down Roger's cheek. "You promised

you weren't leaving me, and I'm holding you to your word."

"Is that…a yes?" Paul's eye's glistened in the harsh light of the room.

Roger nodded as he sniffled. "You bet it is." He rose up again and gently kissed Paul, resisting the urge to embrace him.

Paul slid his free hand along Roger's arm and shoulder, then weakly cupped the back of his head to press their lips firmly together. Paul's hand slipped back down to the bed.

As he broke the kiss, Roger ran his thumb along Paul's cheek. "We need to talk about your family."

Paul turned his head to the side and closed his eyes. "Yeah."

"Did you hear what your sister said to me?" Roger sat back down. He still held tight to Paul's hand, afraid to let go.

"No." He didn't look at Roger.

"She said she missed you." Roger stared hard at his new fiancé. "Paul, they came here to see you. I didn't call your dad, but your mother was so relieved to know where you were."

"They hurt me…real bad." He opened his eyes and faced Roger, his eyes wet and red-rimmed. "He beat me. She walked away."

"What happened after he threw you out the door?"

Paul turned away again, not answering.

Roger kissed his knuckles. "Okay, I won't press you now. You should get some rest. I'll go deal with your family." He lowered Paul's hand back to the sheet.

Returning his sleepy gaze, Paul gave a slight nod. "Come back later?"

He caressed Paul's face and smiled. "I'll be here when you wake up."

With a slow exhale, Paul settled on the pillow and closed his eyes. His face softened into contented sleep.

After a moment, Roger slipped from the room and strode down the hall. Little Pauley played with a toy train on the floor next to his mother and father. The pretty woman gave quiet, encouraging words to her son intermixed with stern glares at her own father. Tasheeka held her arms crossed, the anger flowing off her in waves. Stan sat on the other side of the room slouched over and miserable, clearly banished from the rest of the family.

All four adults perked up when Roger approached. "Paul is resting right now."

Tasheeka stood. "I'll go sit by him."

Rising, Stan strode across the room. "No, I'll do it."

Roger held up his hand, wondering if he needed to call Jason after all. "No. He doesn't want to see either of you right now."

Tasheeka moved forward, but Stan placed a hand on her shoulder. "Leave it, Tasheeka. He doesn't want us."

She recoiled as if a snake had bitten her. Pulling her shoulder away from his grip, she rounded on him. "Keep your hands off me. You ain't my husband no more."

He lifted his hands. "Okay, okay."

"Stop it," Roger snapped. "You're in an ICU ward. Take your domestic squabbles somewhere else."

Paul's parents swung their attention back at him.

Tasheeka snapped her mouth shut, but her glare spoke volumes.

Roger stared her down until she moved back to her chair and plopped down with a huff and crossed arms. After dealing with Marsha Fisher and Jason Lynch earlier that week, neither Tasheeka nor Stan Tomlinson held any fear for him. Mentally rolling his eyes, he addressed the four adults. "I suggest you get settled in your rooms. I have your number, Tasheeka. I'll let you know if and when he wants to speak to you."

Instead of Tasheeka answering, her daughter nodded. "Thank you, Roger. I think that would be best." She stared hard at Tasheeka. "Don't you agree, Mamma?"

Roger took a moment to appreciate Paul's sister. Melia Tomlinson, or whatever her married name was, possessed a quiet fire, much like her brother. Though lighter in complexion, brother and sister shared similar features from both of their parents. Shorter in stature than her mother, her confidence and strength dominated the room as much as her strong-willed parents.

Glancing between Melia and Roger, Tasheeka threw up her hands. "Fine. If that's the way it's gonna be."

Not budging an inch, Roger nodded. "It is." He turned on a heel and strode back to Paul's room, not sparing them another glance.

"ROGER!" PAUL WHEEZED as his eyes sprang open.

Shooting out of the chair, Roger rushed to the bed and took Paul's hand. "I'm here. Are you okay?"

With a deep intake of breath then a puff and a wince, Paul nodded. "Mamma and Dad?"

"They're in the waiting room." He rubbed his thumb along Paul's wrist. "Do you want to see one of them?"

"No." Paul squeezed his eyes closed tight.

"Paul?" Roger said with an even tone. "I need to know more about what happened after they threw you out."

"Can't. Painful," he wheezed.

"Look at me." He cupped Paul's face as his eyes opened. "I'm not going to let them hurt you in any way. Hell, if I call Jason, he'll throw them out onto the street and get a restraining order."

Relaxing somewhat, Paul chuckled then winced. "That hurt."

Concern furrowed Roger's brow. "Do you want me to call the nurse?"

"No...I'm okay."

"We're getting married, Paul. You can't hide this from me." He stared intently. "Is this why you help those street kids? Why you won't talk about your family?" When Paul didn't answer, Roger sat in the chair and pulled his hands away from Paul's cheeks. "Please tell me. I promise it'll stay between the two of us."

"Okay." He sighed, and a grimace tightened his expression. "After I picked myself up from the steps...I limped away with a bloody nose...and a scrape on my leg. My buddy, Jose, and his parents...they took me in...got me patched up."

"Did you stay with them long?"

Paul shook his head. "No. Wouldn't tell them why...I

got thrown out. Was afraid…they'd make me go. Two days. I emptied my bank account…money my grandparents left me… Caught a bus north. Had a scholarship to Miami State…but didn't want to be near them."

"Where did you go?"

"St. Louis." He turned his head away again.

Roger furrowed his brow, concerned at Paul's distress. "What is it?"

"Never told anyone…how I got here." He choked back a sob.

"Paul, you can tell me anything."

"I ran out of money… didn't know what to do." He squeezed his eyes tight again. "I sold myself."

Roger held back his gasp, trying not to react and make his lover feel worse. He could see the shame burning across Paul's face, and it made Roger's heart ache. "Sweetheart, it's okay." And it was. Imagining a teenaged Paul, hungry and desperate, his chest tightened.

"Got enough money together… Got out of St. Louis… Bus to Seattle. As far away…from Florida… as I could get…without a passport." He sniffled as his voice quaked.

"I'm glad you didn't have one." Roger rubbed his thumb along Paul's hand. "I'd have never met you if you had."

Nodding, Paul continued. "I turned tricks downtown. One of the johns…he told me about the police academy… Let me be his houseboy…until I graduated." He turned back to face Roger. "Saved my life."

Roger noted the fear in Paul's eyes. *He doesn't think I*

can handle this. Roger swallowed a lump burning the back of his throat. "Do you know how amazing you are?" Roger marveled at the man before him. The man he was madly in love with. "Beaten, out on the street with no one, and you managed not only to survive, but you didn't self-destruct or turn into a bitter, angry person."

A sob wracked his body as Paul closed his eyes.

"Hey, look at me." Roger let go of Paul's hand and cupped his cheek. "Paul?"

Paul opened his tear-filled eyes.

"You're extraordinary. Kind. Beautiful." Roger caressed his cheek. "I'm so lucky to have you. There's nothing to be ashamed of."

A tear trickled down Paul's cheek, and Roger wiped it away.

"It's okay, sweetheart." Roger leaned down and kissed his forehead. "Now you have a chance to reconcile with your family. They came, and though I think they were completely stupid, they obviously still care about you."

"I don't know, Rog." He exhaled a miserable breath and winced.

"If you want, I'll be right here with you when you talk to them. I'll be your bouncer." He filled out his chest with a deep breath and flexed the sinewy muscles of his arms.

Paul gave a weak laugh. "Fierce." He closed his eyes. "I'll think about it."

"Okay."

ROGER LEFT PAUL'S ROOM after he fell asleep. Still reeling

from his partner's story, Roger stepped into the waiting room to find Paul's father sitting there alone. Unsure what to say to the man, he considered just walking out the door.

"Hey." The man stood, waving a hand at Roger.

With a heavy sigh, Roger stopped. "Yes?"

"I take it you are my son's, uh, partner?" He looked a bit sheepish. "Is that the right word?"

"Yeah. We love each other." Roger stood still, not drawing nearer or giving any warmth to the man, but not discouraging him either.

The older man stared at his feet. "I'm glad he found someone." Bringing his gaze up, he approached Roger and held out his hand. "I'm Stan Tomlinson."

"Roger Matthews." Reluctantly, he shook Stan's hand.

"Do you have a few minutes?" He nodded toward the chairs. "Tasheeka ordered me to tell you she and Melia would be back tomorrow morning."

Roger shrugged. "Okay."

Leading him to two upholstered chairs, Stan motioned him to sit. He took the seat next to Roger. "I don't know how much my son told you about what happened."

Fighting the urge to shout, Roger calmly locked his gaze with Stan's. "He said you gave him a bloody nose and threw him down the front steps with only the clothes on his back, because he told you he's gay." Roger felt no need to sugarcoat his words for Stan.

With a wince, Stan nodded. "Yes." He stared at his shoes again. "I'm not proud of what I did. It took me a long time to get my head out of my ass, and I lost my entire family. You saw my ex-wife's reaction to seeing me today."

"I certainly saw your son's." Roger huffed. "Why did you come here to see him?"

Stan raised his head, his expression raw, his eyes burning. "Believe it or not," he said, his voice hoarse, "I've been looking for him for the last decade. He'd disappeared off the face of the Earth, and I thought I'd never get a chance to make up for my actions." He sat back heavily. "Tasheeka's parents passed on a long time ago, but my mother was alive until last year. She never forgave me, and after Tasheeka told her what I'd done, she disowned and disinherited me."

Roger's frostiness melted somewhat. "So, you've been alone for several years?"

"Yes." He raked a hand through his hair. "I let one drunken day and my own ignorance destroy everything, and no one has given me a second chance. I saw my grandchild for the first time today, and Melia wouldn't let him come near me." He wrung his hands. "I just want a chance to prove I can be a dad to Paulser again."

Sitting back in the chair, Roger sighed. "I've asked Paul to speak to you and his mother, but it's up to him, and I'm going to support whatever he chooses to do." Roger stood, exhausted both mentally and physically. "I need to call our friend to come sit with him while I get some sleep."

Stan sat forward, ready to say something.

Roger held up a hand. "I know you want to help, but he's not ready to see you. Jason can sit with him for now. I've learned over the last two years not to push Paul to do anything."

Bowing his head, Stan slumped in the chair. "You're right. He's pretty stubborn. Always was as a kid."

Pulling out his cell, Roger stepped forward. "Look, I'll take your phone number. Why don't you go get some rest, and if Paul wants to see you, I'll call."

He handed his phone to Paul's father, and Stan programmed in his number. "Thanks." He stood and left the waiting room, shoulders drooping. The scary man from Paul's childhood looked haunted.

Shaking his head, Roger sent a text to Jason. *Can you come sit with P?*

His phone dinged almost immediately. *Ten minutes away. He ok?*

Typing, Roger sat down. *He woke up today. You won't believe the shit show going on here.*

Another ding. *Parking. There soon.*

Roger sat back and closed his eyes. *I wish I didn't have to work tomorrow.*

CHAPTER EIGHT

R OGER DRAGGED HIMSELF into the office early in the morning. Jason and Mike would take turns sitting with Paul for the day while Roger got a shift in. His back still ached from the overnight on the tiny couch in the hospital room, and he'd reluctantly trudged home early in the morning to get changed for work.

The e-mails were the worst part of being away for any length of time. Having only been gone three days, he was dismayed to discover the two hundred plus messages clogging his inbox. Clark had done a fantastic job of keeping the check requests and billings current, but the other longer-term projects sat in his inbox like time bombs waiting to explode.

At ten o'clock, Herrington poked his head into the office. "Good morning. How's your guy?"

Bleary-eyed, Roger looked up from his screen. "He woke up yesterday. I'm glad I was there. Thank you so much for the flexibility."

Herrington shrugged. "I'm surprised to see you today. We've been struggling through without you. Mr. Adamson is good, but he can only be here sporadically. If you're here for a good portion of the day, I could meet with you and let you know the hot button issues. Marsha's on the warpath, but I've given her explicit instructions to leave you alone."

With a frown, Roger turned his chair to fully face Herrington. "What's the issue?"

He waved a hand in the air. "Oh, the usual. She's worried about the implementation of the software package, and whether it will have all the bells and whistles she thinks she needs. Nothing I can't handle."

With a shake of his head, Roger blew out an exasperated breath. "Has she even looked at the specs I sent out before that first meeting?"

His boss smirked. "You mean the presentation where you dressed her down and threatened to quit?"

Heat spread across his face. "Uh, yeah."

"Angelica calls that meeting 'the epic smack down'." Herrington laughed. "I think you'll find Marsha has a lot more respect for you than she ever did before. She's even asked about your partner."

Roger's eyes widened. "Really?"

"Indeed." Herrington glanced at the clock on the wall. "How about ten minutes, and I can fill you in?"

"Sounds good." Roger's cell buzzed in his pocket. "Sorry, do you mind if I get this?"

"Go right ahead. Come find me when you're finished." He turned and left the office.

Roger pulled the cell from his pocket and accepted the call. "This is Roger."

"Hey, babe." Paul's raspy voice made him smile.

Still not quite able to check the emotion that had built

up over the last week, Roger took a deep breath to calm the choking in his voice. "Hi, sweetheart. How are you doing this morning?"

"I'm more alert, I think. Missed you when I woke up."

Roger frowned. "I had to head into work and needed to stop at the condo for a change of clothes."

He paused, and his voice took on a bewildered child's tone. "Did my family really show up yesterday, or was I on a bad drug trip?"

"Yup. Your mother is quite the force of nature." Roger hesitated, wondering if Paul remembered anything else about the prior afternoon's conversation.

Bitterness seeped into his tone. "Can't believe they're here." He paused. "Was I crying yesterday?"

"Yes, but don't worry. I won't tell anyone." Roger chuckled.

He sighed. "Too late. Jason's sitting here. I'm using his phone."

Jason's laugh came through the phone.

Paul's voice turned gruff. "Shut up."

Roger cleared his throat. "Do I need to come and separate you boys?"

With a wheezing chuckle of his own, Paul rasped his response, "Maybe."

"I have to work at least part of the day, but I'll be there as soon as I can get away." Pulling a notepad from his desk drawer, Roger stood and snagged a pen and his coffee cup from the desk.

"I miss you, Rog."

Roger sat on the edge of the desk. "I miss you, too."

Even though he'd been there through the night, he still wished he'd taken another day away from work. He paused again, unsure if he should ask what he wanted to know. Summoning his courage, he pressed forward. "Do you remember anything we talked about after your parents left the room?"

Another chuckle sounded. "You mean me asking you to marry me? You said yes, right?"

"I definitely did." With a sigh of relief, Roger relaxed. "I was hoping you'd remember."

Jason let out a whoop.

Roger grinned. "I guess that tells me what Jason thinks." He stood and headed toward the door. "Have you thought about talking to your family?"

"Yeah." His tone turned serious. "I want my bouncer here. I'm willing to see them, but not without you."

"I'll be there. Do you want me to arrange something?" He opened the cap on the pen and set the pad on his desk.

"Mom first. Not as scary."

Roger thought back to the contrite man in the waiting room, not imagining that he'd be the scary one now after the thunderous storm his mother had unleashed on her ex-husband. Still, this was Paul's show. He'd do anything his sweetheart wanted. "Whatever you want. I can call her at lunch. Do you want to talk to her today?"

He sighed. "Let's get it over with. She's in town."

"Okay, I'll make the arrangements." He made a note on the pad. "What about your dad?"

"Maybe tomorrow." Paul sighed. "Not both the same day."

He wrote on the pad *dad tomorrow* and underlined it. "I've got to meet with my boss. Everyone's asking about you here."

"Tell them I'm okay. I love you."

"I love you, too. See you a little later and get some rest today."

"Okay." The cell beeped twice, and the call disconnected.

Roger took a moment to bask in his boyfriend's affection, and allowed himself a brief surge of joy over the fact Paul's proposal hadn't been drug-induced. Picking up the pad, he stepped into the hallway, pausing at the break room to fill his coffee cup, and then proceeded to his boss's office. Just as he was about to step inside, Angelica Scalione exited her office and spied him.

"Roger!" She hurried over to him. "Are you doing all right?" She looked like she wanted to hug him but was unsure if she should.

"I just spoke with my partner, and he said to say he's getting better."

"Then he's awake," she gushed. "Oh, what a relief." She cast a worried glance at him. "And what about you?"

"I could use a little more sleep, but I'm okay." He glanced in at his boss, and decided to share his news. "Do you have a moment to step inside Mr. Herrington's office? I have something to tell you both."

A shadow passed over her face. "Is this bad news? You're not leaving us, are you?"

Herrington glanced up in alarm.

Roger laughed. "Not at all." He stood aside and let her

enter the office, following and closing the door.

As Angelica took a seat, Herrington arched an eyebrow. "You have something to tell us?"

With a nod, Roger sat in the other chair in front of his boss's desk. "Paul woke up yesterday, and he asked me to marry him. I thought he was delusional from all the drugs, but he told me this morning he meant it. I said yes."

Angelica sprang from her seat with eyes wide and a bright smile on her face. She didn't hold back the hug this time. "That's wonderful news. I'm so happy for you two."

"Indeed." Herrington chuckled. "I hope we're invited."

"Of course." Roger smiled, disentangling himself from the senior partner's embrace. "No details yet. Paul's still in the ICU, but we'll see how it goes. I'm hoping to speak to the doctors about his prognosis this afternoon."

"Well, we'll keep it to ourselves until you're ready to tell the rest of the office. Right, Angelica?" Herrington leveled a stern gaze at her.

"Don't worry, Herrington. I can keep my mouth shut." She turned back to Roger, her eyes sparkling with excitement. "If you need any help planning, just let me know."

Herrington cleared his throat. "Okay, Angelica. I only have this young man for a few hours, so we need to make the most of his time."

She moved toward the door. "I won't keep you." She turned the knob. "You'll probably want to mention it to Marsha. Her new-found respect for you would only increase if you tell her something like that in confidence."

She winked and left the room.

"Let's get through a few things. If you finish up before one, you're welcome to head to Harborview."

HAPPY AT HAVING completed the projects his boss had laid out for him, Roger hurried up James Street. Though the wind swirled around him, he barely noticed the cold. He pressed the contact for Paul's mother on his cell and held the phone to his ear.

She answered after the first ring. "Roger?"

"Hi, Ms. Tomlinson."

"Honey, please. Call me Tasheeka."

Her voice sounded equal parts fear and hope. "Paul asked me to call you and see if you'd be willing to talk."

"What time?"

Her immediate response didn't surprise him at all. Roger glanced at the screen of the cell and returned it to his ear. "It's about one-thirty now. Why don't you come by at four?"

"Okay, we'll be there." She paused. "Thank you, Roger. I just want my baby back."

"Your ex-husband said the same thing to me last night. See you at four." He ended the call before she could comment further. He hadn't heard the story of what happened to their marriage, but he surmised Stan Tomlinson's drunken beating of her son destroyed their relationship.

He reached Ninth Avenue and turned right one block from the hospital entrance. An ambulance screamed by, siren blaring. As he approached the main doors, Jason caught up to him.

"Hey, Roger. I didn't expect to see you so early." His smile was genuine as he accompanied Roger into the lobby.

Roger was glad to see him. "My boss let me out early. How's he looking today?"

"Good." They stepped to the elevator bay, and Jason pressed the button. "He has more color back in his face."

The doors slid open, and they stepped onto the car. Roger's chest fluttered as he considered what was going to happen later in the afternoon. The ride to the basement was quick, and they stepped off the elevator, heading down the hall toward the ward.

"What's up, Roger? You look worried." Jason's brow furrowed.

"Tasheeka Tomlinson is coming later to meet with her son. Other than when he first woke up and demanded that she and his father leave, Paul hasn't seen his family in over fifteen years."

Jason puffed out a breath. "I heard him say he'd be willing to talk to her. Is it a good idea to do it while he's in the ICU?"

Roger shrugged. "I don't know. His family is all here. I'm not sure it's fair to deny them the chance if Paul's willing."

With a frown, Jason shook his head. "But is it going to be too stressful for him?"

Something he was worried about, too. "At the first sign they're upsetting him, I'll throw them out myself."

His nostrils flared as he considered the many ways things could go wrong. He calmed himself as they entered the waiting area. "I get the feeling they want this to work. His parents want him back in their lives. Why else would they have spent the money to come out to Seattle? It couldn't have been cheap at short notice."

Jason walked him to the door of Paul's room. "If you need anything, text me, and I'll lend you some police muscle."

"Are you back on duty?"

The smile returned to Jason's face. "Yeah. It didn't take long to wrap up the investigation. The witnesses all said the shooting was justified, so I'm cleared to return to patrol duty."

Roger stepped into Paul's room with Jason following. Mike rose from the chair and approached. "He's resting. I think the doctor wanted to talk to you, Roger."

A surge of apprehension gripped Roger as he glanced over at his partner, who was peacefully sleeping. "Is there something wrong?"

Mike shook his head. "I don't think so. Probably just to update you."

Nodding at both of their friends, Roger left the room and strode to the nurse's station. The woman at the desk looked up.

"Hi, I heard that Dr. Sakurai wanted to speak to me?"

The nurse checked her screen. "Yes. She's available. Let me get her." The woman stood and stepped to an open office door. "Paulser Tomlinson's partner is here."

Dr. Sakurai followed the charge nurse out of the office

and came around the front of the desk. "Roger, right?"

"Yes. How is he?"

She smiled. "He's improving rapidly. I'm planning to have him transferred to one of the wards upstairs."

Relief rolled over him. "That's good news. When do you think he can come home?"

"If all goes well, he'll likely be released by the weekend." Her gaze locked with his. "It's not going to be an easy transition for him."

"What do you mean?"

Her smile turned sad. "I don't think he's going to be out on his beat anytime soon. I think I mentioned to you and Officer Lynch that here was extensive damage in his chest. One of the bullets flattened and tore him up. The lung is still struggling to function properly. He won't be able to stand too much physical exertion. You'll have to watch him carefully."

Roger's resolve hardened. He'd do whatever he needed to ensure Paul made it back to full health. "That's not going to be a problem."

Her brow furrowed. "I understand his estranged family is here."

Roger frowned. "Yes. The first meeting didn't go well, but I think Paul was more surprised than angry to see them."

"Will they be back?"

With a sigh, Roger nodded. "His mother is coming in this afternoon, maybe with his sister."

"I can check and see if the caseworker assigned to Officer Tomlinson is available if you need some help. She may be able to suggest some counseling options."

"Let's wait and see how the initial meeting goes. I'm hopeful the parents will be easier to deal with separately."

She shifted her weight on her feet. "If possible, don't let him get upset. He shouldn't move around much, and stress or anger wouldn't be good for his recovery."

Roger regretted calling Paul's mother even more, but this situation probably couldn't have been avoided with the HR person at the SPD calling Stan Tomlinson. He'd have to make sure once Paul was out of the hospital that the emergency contact information for both of them stated not to call family without the expressed permission of the partner.

Addressing the doctor, Roger nodded. "Officer Lynch has offered to be a bouncer if I need him. I think he called it *police muscle*."

She chuckled. "He seems like a toughie."

"Yeah," Roger mused, "but he's a nice guy. I'd better get back to Paul."

"If you need anything, let the nurse know. We've got a good crew on this afternoon." She returned to her office as Roger strode down the hallway to Paul's room.

He paused in the doorway, catching a glimpse of Jason and Mike seated and looking at Paul. Mike had his head on Jason's shoulder, and they held each other's hand. Jason had his arm slung around his husband's shoulder. The sight made Roger long to feel Paul's arms around him again, strong and protective.

Catching a glimpse of Roger in the doorway, Mike lifted his head and stood. "Hey, how did it go with the doctor?"

"He's going to need some rehab work." He shifted his gaze to Jason. "You might need another beat partner for a while."

With a shrug, Jason also stood. "Just can't keep good help. First Fred, and now Paul."

Mike chuckled. "I suppose I'll have to help Fred beat the Templetons at pool."

With a sharp breath, Paul shifted on the bed. "Thought so. You're just waiting to take my spot."

Raising his hands, Mike turned to Paul. "Hey, I'm just helping out. Fred will have a nervous breakdown if he can't compete in the SPD Pool Tournament."

"Hmm…" Paul frowned. "You can if I can watch."

Mike smirked. "Why Officer Tomlinson, I didn't know you were such a voyeur."

The four men all chuckled.

Roger stepped to the bed and laced his fingers with Paul's. "How are you feeling, sweetheart?" Looking over his lover, Roger was relieved to see the usual umber color of Paul's skin no longer chalky and pale, and there was much more clarity in his eyes.

"Breathing isn't easy." Paul sighed. "How long am I stuck here?"

Jason rolled his eyes. "If he's already complaining about the accommodations, he must be doing better."

"The doctor just told me she's very happy with your progress and is considering transferring you to a different room." Roger patted his shoulder. "At least you'll be out of the ICU."

"That's an improvement," Paul replied glumly. He stared into Roger's eyes. "I want to go home with you."

"I'd rather *have* you at home, but I can't give you the care you need until you're better."

"I know." Paul glanced at Jason and Mike. "Do you guys mind giving us a few minutes alone?"

Mike nodded. "No problem. Come on, Jase."

After the two men left the room and closed the door, Roger pulled up the chair next to Paul's bed. "What's up, sweetheart?"

Paul reached out a hand to grasp Roger's. "I'm scared. About talking to Mamma."

The big, tough cop rarely admitted fear, so Roger sat up straighter in the chair determined to allay his concern.

"Give her a chance. I have a feeling this is going to turn out much better than you think." He squeezed Paul's hand. "She sounded so hopeful when I talked to her. They've been looking for you for years. Even your dad."

"I didn't want them to find me." Paul shut his eyes and pushed his head back into the pillow.

"Why?"

Squeezing his lids tighter, Paul's voice cracked. "They'd hurt me again."

Roger used his other hand to rub along Paul's arm. "They spent a lot of money to come out here. I only called your mother the day before yesterday, and she was here the next day. That doesn't sound like something they'd do just to come here and cause problems."

Paul turned to stare at Roger with glistening eyes. "You'll be here with me?"

"Of course." He brought Paul's hand to his mouth and kissed along the knuckles. "Let's agree on a signal if you want me to haul them out of here."

"I could tug on my earlobe." Paul used his free hand to slowly reach up and grab the lobe. He gave a quick pull and dropped his hand back onto the bed.

"The second I see you do that, I'll drag your mom out of here." His brow furrowed at the thought of pulling Tasheeka Tomlinson away from her son. "Jason can help me if I can't make her go." With a final kiss, Roger set Paul's hand back on the sheet. "I'm sure it won't come to that. She wants this to work."

Sighing, Paul stared at the ceiling. "Let's get this over with. When's she coming?"

AT FOUR O'CLOCK sharp, Roger stepped from Paul's room and strode to the waiting area. Jason sat in a chair reading a book. He looked up as Roger took the seat next to him.

"Thanks for staying."

Jason dog-eared the page he was on and set the book on the table next to him. "No problem. How's he doing?"

Roger frowned. "He's terrified this will go badly." With a heavy sigh, Roger sat back. "I really don't know if I did the right thing calling her."

Turning in his chair, Jason faced him full on. "Hey, you took a chance. If this goes well, Paul's going to have his family back."

"And if it doesn't?" Roger stared at the officer. "What then?"

Jason shrugged and counted each point on his fingers. "One, Paul will know where he stands. Two, they'll have missed the opportunity to make things right. And three, you all move on with your lives."

The elevator doors opened, and Tasheeka Tomlinson stepped off the elevator with Melia and little Pauley in tow.

"Show time," Roger muttered as he stood.

Paul's mother pulled Roger into a hug as she reached them, nearly crushing him in her embrace. "Thank you."

Roger patted her back and pulled away. "Ready?"

"I hope so." She turned to her daughter. "Honey, you wait here while I talk to Paulser."

"Okay, Mamma." Melia set Pauley down, and he scampered over to a pile of toys in the corner of the waiting room. She chased after him. "What did you find, Pauley?"

Roger led Tasheeka down the hallway and into his partner's room then stepped to the side, allowing her to pass and approach the bed. With a scrape along the tiled floor, Roger pushed a chair next to the bed for her.

She smiled her thanks and took a seat. Then her gaze rested on her son, whose expression was taut and whose gaze reflected apprehension. "Paulser, the first thing you need to know is I'm so sorry I wasn't there to protect you from your father."

Watching for the agreed upon signal, Roger leaned against the doorway and eyed Tasheeka. While he hoped for Paul's sake things went well, he'd in no way let her upset Paul.

Paul glared at her from the bed. "You just turned and walked away like I was garbage."

"I never thought you were garbage. Ever. But I needed time to process what you'd said. I was in shock." She returned his glare with a fierce determination of her own. "I failed you, but I never stopped loving you. Melia and I both tried to find you, but you'd disappeared."

"I was on the streets for a long time." He cast a furtive glance at Roger but didn't give the signal. Instead, the look on his face conveyed his fear Roger might reveal the rest of the story.

Roger placed his hand on his heart and gave a single shake of his head. Surely Paul knew he'd never reveal something spoken in confidence. He'd already done enough by calling Tasheeka. The rest was up to Paul.

Returning his gaze to his mother, Paul seemed reassured. Slowly, the tension in his face faded. "So, what now?" he asked, then swallowed. "We just pretend like nothing happened, like every other uncomfortable moment in our family?"

"Paulser, I'm not the scared woman I was when you were a teenager." She glanced over at Roger. "Your friend tells me your father is also trying to be a better person." She turned back and reached for him, but hesitated and returned her hand to her lap.

With a frown, Paul stared at the ceiling, not meeting her gaze.

"Honey, I can't undo what's been done. But your wonderful young man has given us a second chance." She reached out again, and this time she took his hand. He didn't pull away.

Heat rushed to Roger's checks as he realized she meant him.

"This family has been broken without you, Paulser. We need you back. Little Pauley needs an uncle." She squeezed her son's hand. "Melia and I have missed you so much." She sniffled, tears flowing unchecked down her cheeks.

"I can't forget what happened." Paul's lip trembled, but Roger resisted the urge to go to him.

"You don't have to forget. Just let it go. It's past. It's dead." She shook her head. "Those people are gone. Melia's an adult with a child. I'm not with your father anymore, and I'm finally my own person. I haven't seen him in years. Before yesterday, that is."

A tear trickled out of the corner of Paul's eye. Roger clenched his fists but stayed rooted in place, wanting nothing more than to fling his arms around his partner and hold him.

"How do I know you won't turn your back on me again?" Paul faced his mother, indecision clear in his handsome face.

Tasheeka sucked in a ragged breath. "I swear I'll never walk away again. Just give me a chance to show you."

With a single nod, Paul choked back a sob. His mother rose to her feet and leaned over his bed, carefully hugging her son close. He wrapped his arms around her.

A wave of relief washed over Roger.

Little feet pattered from the hallway into the room. "Gam-ma!"

Roger glanced at the doorway and found little Pauley charging his way inside with a bright-eyed smile, diaper pushing out of the elastic of his little jeans. Melia burst into the room after him. "Come here, stinker. It's not our turn."

Rising out of the embrace, Tasheeka wiped her eyes and held out her hands. "It's okay. Come to grandma, sugarplum."

As Pauley rushed into his grandmother's embrace with a happy squawk, Roger stepped around Tasheeka and grabbed a couple tissues for Paul. He leaned down and placed a kiss on Paul's cheek as he pushed the Kleenex into his hand. "I'm so proud of you, sweetheart."

Paul sniffled, clearing his throat. "Something's in my eye."

Moving his lips to his lover's ear and lowering his voice, Roger leaned closer. "When you get sprung from this place, I'm going to do some very naughty things to help with your physical therapy."

With a hiss of breath, Paul's eyes widened. "Not while my family's here."

Chuckling, Roger nodded. "Okay. I'll go into detail later."

Tasheeka stepped closer, carrying little Pauley. "He's a handful."

Standing, Roger backed away a couple steps, but Paul held out his hand. Roger clasped it, staying close by the bed.

With a squeeze of his hand, Paul addressed his mother and Melia. "I asked Roger to marry me yesterday."

Both of the women's eyes widened, but Roger noted it wasn't shock or disgust. The grins plastered on their faces spoke volumes. Tasheeka glanced at Melia and then to Roger. "And did you give him an answer?"

"I told him I'd think about it," Roger deadpanned.

Her eyebrow arched. "Is that so?"

With a laugh, Roger shook his head. "I said yes, though I was a little worried it was the painkillers asking."

Paul pulled Roger's hand to his lips and kissed his knuckles. "I already have the ring. If I hadn't gotten myself shot, I'd have asked him on his birthday."

Melia clapped her hands. "I'm so happy for you, big brother."

A knock at the door caught their attention. Dr. Sakurai stood in the doorframe, a smile on her face. "Looks like things went well."

Roger nodded. "Better than I'd hoped."

"I've put through the order to have Officer Tomlinson moved to a more comfortable room upstairs." She directed her attention to Paul. "We're very happy with your progress, and I feel we can upgrade you from critical to serious condition and free you from the basement."

Paul grinned. "Things are definitely looking up."

Sharing his smile, Roger nodded. Though relieved the conversation had gone so well with Tasheeka, Stan was still waiting for his turn tomorrow.

CHAPTER NINE

LATER IN THE early evening, Roger took in the spectacular view from the window of Paul's new room. Dr. Sakurai had arranged for a private room overlooking Puget Sound and the Olympic Mountains. The clear spring day gave way to a glorious sunset with pink wispy clouds fanning across the snow-capped peaks. The pink was also reflected in the shimmering waters of the Sound.

Paul stared out the window as well. "Should've kept me in ICU."

Sitting in a chair next to his lover, Roger furrowed his brow. "Why's that?"

"Wouldn't know what I'm missing outside." He kept his gaze fixed on the setting sun. "It's not gonna go so well with Dad."

Roger took Paul's hand, careful to avoid the attached IV. "Do you want me to tell him not to come tomorrow?"

He grimaced. "I don't know. I keep going back to the day he threw me out." With a sigh, he focused on Roger. "Even if he's changed, he still brutalized and abandoned me to the streets."

"I suppose." Roger considered before asking the next

question that came to his mind. While he didn't want to upset Paul, he had to know whether or not to tell Stan Tomlinson to stay away. "Are you still the same boy he threw out?"

"No. I wish I could tell my younger self everything was going to be okay." He shrugged, but his voice grew angry. "He blew up his family just because he had a gay son."

Roger squeezed his hand, worried Paul would have some sort of reaction to the stress. "How many street kids have you sent to the non-profit Clark works for?"

"Too many. I feel it every time I find a gay kid shivering in a doorway or cowering underneath an overpass. Now, you know why." He placed a hand over his chest, his mouth tightening into a line.

Roger sat up straighter. "Are you okay?"

"Yeah, just some pain. Maybe the oxy wore off." Paul sucked in a sharp breath. "Actually, you better get someone."

Bolting for the door as chilly panic washed over him, Roger called over his shoulder. "I'll be right back." He caught a nurse as he was about to go into another patient's room. "Officer Tomlinson's having some chest pains."

The nurse nodded. "I'll get the charge nurse." He hurried down the corridor toward the nurse's station.

Roger returned to Paul's side. "Someone will be here soon."

Lifting his right hand, Paul grimaced and reached out. "Roger."

Just as Roger grasped his hand, the charge nurse calmly stepped into the room. Her nametag showed her name as Monique. She came to the other side of the bed from Roger and took Paul's wrist. "How are you doing, Officer Tomlinson?"

"My chest feels like someone is squeezing it with a vice." He grimaced again.

"When did you have your last pain medication?" She checked his pulse and moved to the computer on the retractable arm.

Roger kept a hold of Paul's hand. "The last one was while he was still in the ICU, I think around one o'clock."

"You're due." She looked over the screen and turned to Paul. "Your pulse is racing, but it doesn't look like you're having a heart attack." She lay a hand on his arm. "Take a few deep breaths. Can you do that for me?"

With a nod, Paul closed his eyes and took a breath. Though he winced as he did, he let the air out in a long, even stream. He took another and did the same.

"How's your chest feeling now?" She patted his bicep and returned to the computer screen.

"Hurts, but the tightness isn't as bad." Paul took in another deep breath and released it.

She checked his pulse again. "Better. Your heartbeat is a little slower." She headed for the door. "I'm going to get your pain meds. I'll be right back."

Paul nodded.

With his own heartbeat thundering in his head, Roger kept hold of Paul's hand and leaned in, resting his forehead against Paul's hair, relief calming his fear. "You better not die on me. I don't even have my ring."

Chuckling and then gasping, Paul squeezed Roger's

hand. "I'm okay. Not leaving you yet."

"You better not ever leave me." Roger held on tight to Paul and tried to calm his own racing heart.

Monique returned with a packet. She scanned the barcode on the wrapper then tore it open. Pouring the two pills into a small cup, she passed it to Paul. "Take these."

Roger stood and grabbed a glass of water with a straw, passing it to Paul after he popped the pills onto his tongue. Paul took several swallows then nodded.

After tossing the packaging into the trashcan next to the computer, Monique glanced at her patient again. "How are you doing now?"

"Better, thanks. Still hurts, though."

She patted his arm one more time and headed for the door. "The medication will take effect soon. If you have any more pain, you let me know right away. Don't try to tough it out."

Roger let go of Paul's hand. "I'll be right back, okay?"

"Sure." Paul closed his eyes.

Following the nurse into the hallway, Roger caught her before she could go back down the hall. "What happened to him?"

"A mild anxiety attack. He wasn't showing signs of a heart attack. Was he upset about anything?"

Roger nodded. "We've been having some family drama. They showed up yesterday after throwing him out fifteen years ago."

She whistled. "Well, that would do it. He's been through quite a lot in the last few days, what with being shot and his stint in the ICU. His body isn't up for a lot of stress yet."

"I understand. Things went well with his mother, but Paul's worried about dealing with his dad."

"Maybe you should wait a few days to subject him to anymore drama. Did Dr. Sakurai offer the help of a case worker?"

Roger nodded. "Yes."

"You might take her up on it. Let me check and see if Lisa Steiner is available. She's really good with contention between family members."

"Thank you." Roger returned to the room as Monique stepped across the hallway and into another room.

Paul turned his head as Roger entered. "Hey."

"Feeling better?" Roger asked as he pulled the chair to the side of the bed and sat.

With a nod, Paul adjusted the bed so he sat up a little straighter.

Hesitating, Roger considered his words carefully. "The nurse suggested finding a counselor to mediate between you and your dad. What do you think?"

Paul frowned. "I don't know, Rog. I don't like other people knowing too much about my business." Paul reached for his hand again. "Thanks for not saying anything about my hustling."

"Sweetheart, I'd never betray any confidence you tell me." Roger squeezed his hand. "But maybe you'll want to tell them an abridged version at some point."

He shook his head. "Mamma and Melia don't need to know."

Roger shrugged. "They're going to ask what happened

to you after you left home. The subject was already broached."

A knock at the door startled Roger, and he turned to find his parents standing at the entrance to the room. His mother beamed as she carried in a bouquet of tulips in a glass vase. "Paul, we are so relieved you're okay."

His father followed her in and approached the bed. "How are you doing, son?" He placed a hand on Paul's shoulder.

Paul's smile brightened the room. "I'll be just fine, sir, thank you." He addressed Roger's mother. "The flowers are beautiful, Nora."

She set the vase onto the table next to the window and stepped around the bed to Roger, holding out her arms. "Hi, honey."

Roger stood, reaching out and hugging her. "Hi, Mom."

Holding him at arm's length after a moment, she stared into his face. A worried frown tugged at her lips. "You look exhausted, honey. Have you been sleeping?"

Roger glanced at Paul. "It's hard to sleep without Paul being home."

She gave him another squeeze and stepped away. "That's understandable." She patted his arm and nodded at the chair. "Now, sit back down and rest."

"Actually," Paul interjected. "Come stand by me, Rog." He glanced at Roger's parents. "We have some news."

Her eyebrows shot up. "Yes?"

His pulse racing again, Roger returned to Paul's side

and took his hand. He stared deeply into the dark eyes of his partner before addressing his parents. "Paul and I are getting married."

Bringing her hands to her mouth, his mother's eyes watered. "Oh, boys, I'm so happy for you." She threw her arms around Roger. "I hoped you moving in together meant this was coming." She let him go and took Paul's hand. "You're already part of our family, but I'm thrilled it will soon be official."

Roger's father grinned from ear to ear. He also gave Roger a hug. "Congratulations, son."

"Thanks, Dad." Roger marveled at the reception his parents gave Paul and the full acceptance they continued to show him. He and Paul's families were night and day in how they'd treated their sons.

"Of course, I'm sure you boys already know what you want for a wedding," his mother gushed. "But if you want help, I'm at your disposal. We'll help pay for the party as well."

"Mom, I can't ask you to do that." Roger shook his head, his pride flaring, much as it had when Jason accused him of freeloading. "You two should be traveling and using your money for yourselves."

She put her hands on her hips. "Honey, we only have one child, and I set aside funds for both your college and your wedding years ago. Isn't that right, Eric?"

His father nodded. "That's right, son. We planned to help when the day came."

Paul cleared his throat, and they all turned to him. "We're both grateful for your help. Thanks very much."

He placed his hand on his chest.

Outnumbered, Roger frowned but nodded. "Yes, thank you. We'll figure out what we're going to do and let you know. Paul only asked me yesterday, and he's got some time yet for his recovery. It might be a little bit before we can really do any major planning."

His mother's smile returned. "Well, we'll look forward to helping you boys." She narrowed her eyes, poking a painted fingernail at them. "And no skimping on the festivities."

"Not to worry, Nora. We're gonna do it up in style." Paul grinned at her.

She grinned. "I expect nothing less."

ROGER STRODE DOWN SIXTY-FIFTH AVENUE NE to the pub where Paul usually played pool with his coworkers. Tasheeka and Melia had shown up shortly after his parents had left, and Paul had insisted he take the evening and meet up with Clark. He'd stopped off at the condo and grabbed his car, driving the two miles to find the street completely full of parked vehicles. He didn't mind the walk from the parking spot three streets away from the pub.

As he neared the entrance, he waved at his friend hurrying up the street toward him.

Clark waved back. "Hey, Roger. Thanks for meeting me."

"Are you kidding? You've been absolutely amazing. My boss wants me to hire you." He chuckled. "But I know you have a great gig, and I wouldn't dream of trying to pull you away from the Center."

Clark laughed. "You couldn't pay me enough to leave those kids behind. I think I have the most rewarding job in the city." His friend glanced around. "Where did you park?"

"In the neighborhood, but I'm about three blocks away on one of the side streets." Holding open the door, Roger swept out his arm. "At least, let me buy you dinner."

"Now that you can do."

They stepped into the crowded pub and made their way to the bar. Seb grinned as he saw them approach. He gave Roger a nod. "Hey, stranger. I wasn't sure I'd see you again."

Jason sidled up to the bar. "That was totally my fault." He turned to Roger. "Paul doing okay?"

"Yeah, his mom and sister are sitting with him this evening. He insisted I take the night off, but I'll go back after dinner." Roger turned to his companion. "I think you've met my friend, Clark Adamson."

When Clark narrowed his eyes and crossed his arms, Roger could see another round of drama heading his direction.

Jason cocked his head to the side. "Nice to see you again, Clark."

"Debatable." Clark turned his attention to the board above Seb's head advertising the various beers. "I'll have a Bodi with a wedge of lemon."

With the tension palpable, Jason glanced at Roger

with a furrowed brow. "What's eating him?"

Roger sighed. "Clark's still sore at you for what happened the last time I was here."

Looking like he'd been hit with a baseball bat, Jason spluttered. "Roger, I meant my apology. I don't think you're a freeloader, I swear."

Before Roger could respond, Clark swung a wicked glare at Jason. "Pretty words, Officer Asshole. If you didn't mean it, you shouldn't have said it in the first place."

"Clark! Geez!" Roger clapped his hands between them. "I already told you we're good. I appreciate your loyalty, but get over it. Jason's been amazing through this whole ordeal."

Sliding off the barstool, Jason shoved his hands into the pocket of his jeans. "I'm gonna head back to Mike. He's probably wondering where I am."

Roger placed a hand on Jason's shoulder. "No, wait." He frowned at Clark. "Apologize. That was completely uncalled for."

Lifting his eyebrow, the look Clark shot Roger was not one of contrition. "Actions speak louder than words. I know you've given him a pass on what he said to you because Paul's in the hospital, but what he implied was just plain rude. You're a lot more forgiving than I am, Roger."

"I know I fucked up, Clark." Jason shot him a glare. "Roger was very gracious to accept my apology, and I've done my best to be available for both him and Paul."

"Look, Lynch. If Roger wants to forgive and forget because of Paul being in the hospital, that's his business."

Clark narrowed his eyes. "But would you have offered your apology if Paul were still out on the beat?"

"Paul was trying to help me figure out how to make amends when he was shot," Jason replied through gritted teeth. "And if you're implying that I was just exploiting an emotional situation to assuage my guilt, I'll have you know I lost a partner to cancer nine years ago. I know what it's like to have your lover non-responsive in a hospital bed, and I'd *never* take advantage of anyone in a situation like I had to endure."

Clark's face fell, though he still didn't seem convinced of Jason's sincerity. "I'm sorry. That had to be difficult."

"It was the worst experience of my life, and that's saying something." He glanced over to where Mike was chatting with Fred Collier. "Mike helped me realize I could keep going, and Paul made sure I knew I was accepted here in Seattle. Both are very important to me, and I got overprotective of Paul."

Seb brought Clark his beer and turned to Roger and Jason. "What do you guys want to drink?"

Turning away from Clark, Jason sat back at the bar. "I'll have another IPA."

"I'll do a ginger beer." Roger shrugged at Clark's sideways frown. "Gotta keep a clear head to drive back to Harborview later."

With a nod, Seb headed to the taps to draw Jason's beer.

Returning his attention to Clark, Jason fixed him with a hard stare. "It's fine if you have a problem with me. I got my ass handed to me by both Mike and Paul over my stupidity, and I've made my peace with Roger. I think we're good, so that's what is most important to me."

"Yes, Jason." Roger nodded. "We're good. Clark?" He turned to his friend, annoyed but understanding where he was coming from. Clark was the most fiercely loyal friend he'd ever had. If he hadn't been distracted by tater tots, they should have met somewhere else. Still, best to get the animosity out in the open and hopefully dealt with. With their engagement, neither Paul nor Roger needed bad blood between their friends. Clark, whether he knew it or not, needed to keep on the good side of the SPD, considering the interaction his Center had with the force, and that included staying friendly with Officer Jason Lynch.

After a sip of his beer, Clark sighed. "Okay, Jason. I'll take you at your word. Roger's a good friend, and I don't take kindly to anyone who hurts or insults him. He's a hardworking and kind man. Give him that credit, and we'll get along."

Jason nodded. "Deal."

Seb brought their drinks. "I'll keep a tab open for you guys. Any food?"

Snatching a menu from the small metal clip next to the salt and pepper shakers, Roger skimmed the list then handed the paper to Clark. "I don't know why I even look. Steak and brie pie with a mountain of tater tots."

With a shrug, Clark replaced the menu. "I'll have the same with a salad instead of the tots."

Roger shot him a look of surprise. The Clark he knew loved greasy pub food, *especially* tater tots.

"Dressing?" Seb asked.

"Oil and vinegar." Clark glanced at the other two guys and wrinkled his nose. "The doctor says I have to watch it. I also need to keep trim for my sister's wedding."

Roger's eyes widened. "Did Grace say yes to that lout?" Now it was Roger's turn to be protective. Grace Adamson's fiancé, Dan Palucinski, was hardly who he'd envisioned for his best friend's sister. With all of her advocacy, Roger failed to understand what she saw in that loudmouthed frat boy jerk.

After another draw from his pint, Clark grimly nodded. "I don't know what she's thinking marrying that homophobic dumbass—but whatever. I just have to show up."

"You taking a date?" Jason asked and took a swig of his IPA.

"Kind of." The frown on Clark's face didn't bode well for his prospects.

Roger fixed his gaze on his friend, puzzled by his evasive response. "Kind of? What does that mean? Either you are or you aren't."

"Since my best friend, here, wouldn't commit when I asked him three weeks ago, I had to figure something else out," Clark huffed. "Don't worry about it. I'll be fine."

Jason came to Clark's rescue, conveniently changing the subject. "Hey, why don't we join Mike?" he said, pointing his thumb over his shoulder. "He's looking my direction, and you'd be welcome to share the table with us."

"Sound good to you, Clark?" Roger eyed his friend.

With another shrug, Clark nodded. "Fine by me."

As they pushed themselves off the barstools, Roger caught Seb's attention. "We're heading over to Jason and Mike's table."

Seb gave a thumbs-up and went back to taking another customer's order.

They wove their way between full tables to where Mike was sitting. He rose in greeting. "Hi, Roger. Clark, right?" With his patented goofy grin, Mike stuck out his hand.

Clark shook it. "Right. Nice to see you again, Mike."

The hug Mike gave him made Roger smile.

"You doing okay?" Mike asked, his voice gruff and his gaze searching his face.

"Yeah. Paul's on the mend, and that's got me pretty happy." He released Mike. "Clark's been amazing doing my job, keeping things afloat while I've been at the hospital."

Jason gave a low whistle. "Have you figured out how to deal with the infamous Marsha Fisher?"

Laughing, Clark pulled out a chair and sat as the others took their own seats. "She loves a good story, and I have plenty of bullshit to feed her. I really like the other director, Angelica Scalione, and the receptionist is a rock star."

"Yeah, Elsibeth's a sweetie," Roger agreed. He took a sip of his ginger beer.

Seb dodged a backing-out chair and set their plates of food in front of them. "Here you go, guys. Ketchup's on the table. Let me know if you need anything else."

Roger smiled, the aroma of the meat pie making his stomach rumble. "Looks great. Thanks, Seb."

Grinning back, Seb turned and headed toward the bar.

Roger unwrapped the fork and knife from the napkin and stabbed two of the tater tots. He popped them into his mouth and immediately regretted it as the hot potatoes burned his tongue. Huffing air and moving the tots around on his tongue, he quickly swallowed then felt the burn in his throat. He snatched up his drink to put out the fire.

The table erupted in laughter.

Clark shook his head with a grin. "You do that every time, I swear."

"Can't help it," Roger said as the heat in his throat and stomach subsided. He took another draw from his glass. "They're so good, and I'm hungry."

"You can't taste them if you burn off your taste buds," Mike said with a snort.

Jason elbowed his husband and turned to Roger. "Anyway, how's Paul doing with the reappearance of his family?"

Dread settled over him as he stared down at his food. Lifting the ketchup bottle from the table, he popped the lid and hit the side of the jar with his palm until a large dollop plopped around the tots. Though he'd been freaked out about Paul's mother and how things would go with her son, the real test was Paul's father.

"He had a rough start with his mom, but it turned out okay." Roger dipped one of the tots into the ketchup and popped the more reasonably warm morsel into his mouth.

Mike sipped his beer and set the pint on the table. "What about his dad?"

"He's coming in tomorrow afternoon." He looked at each of the guys in turn. "The anxiety attack after he moved rooms scared me. Frankly, I'm worried the meeting with his father isn't going to go well." With his fork, Roger broke open the pastry covering of the meat pie and let the steam rise.

Jason sighed. "I can be there if you want. I don't mind taking the time off."

"Nah, I think I can handle it." He remembered Tasheeka's reaction to seeing her ex-husband at the door of Paul's room and took heart. "If nothing else, Paul's mother would happily rip his father's balls off if things get out of hand."

Chapter Ten

AFTER SPENDING THE morning at the office, Roger returned to Harborview half an hour before the scheduled arrival of Stan Tomlinson. He'd been on edge all day, running through different scenarios in his mind—all of them bad. As he arrived outside the door of Paul's room, he froze in his tracks.

"Paulser, please. I'm a different person. I just want—" Stan's voice drifted into the hallway.

"There's no change. You look older but sound exactly the same." Paul's voice, edged with an icy anger, cut across his father's.

Roger's worst fears seemed realized. The meeting wasn't going well, but he wasn't sure if he should intervene or let Paul handle his dad alone.

With a heavy sigh, Stan continued. "I just want a chance to try and make up for what I did."

"What makes you think I want you in my life? I didn't need you the last fifteen years." Paul's voice rose in volume. "You hurt me. You beat your only son. I had *nothing* when you tossed me to the curb."

"I was wrong. And stupid. And drunk." Desperation crept into Stan's voice. "I don't have anyone left, Paulser.

Your grandmother never forgave me, and she died last year. I never got a chance to reconcile with her."

The tone of Paul's response, low and dangerous, chilled Roger. "If she couldn't forgive you, why should I?"

Paul's voice caught, and Roger's heart ached. He paused outside with his hand on the door, ready to push it the rest of the way open, but waiting to be sure.

"I had nothing and no one," Paul said, his voice thickening. "I had to fucking sell my body, because it was the only way I could survive."

Stan gasped. "I had no idea. I tried to find you. I swear I tried, son. I even kept the old phone number in case you called."

"I didn't *want* you to find me!" Paul roared. "You weren't going to have another chance to hurt me." Paul took in a sharp breath. "Aaah…"

Roger shoved open the door and raced into the room. "Paul?"

His lover clutched at his chest, his eyes wide and mouth open, gasping for air.

Standing by the bed, Stan reached for his son, but Paul batted his hands away as he began to thrash on the bed. "No, get away from me," Paul wheezed.

"Oh, God, Paulser. I'm so sorry." Stan stepped back, terror on his face as he stared helplessly at his writhing son.

Pulse racing, Roger pressed the call button on the remote attached to the bed and then grabbed Stan Tomlinson's arm. "Come on. Outside."

"But, Paulser…" Stan stumbled away from his son as Roger pulled him into the hallway.

"Stay here. He's having an anxiety attack. You should have waited for me before going in." Roger glanced down the hall to the nurse's station and waved at Monique. The nurse saw him and hurried toward them. Knowing she'd be there in moments, Roger returned to Paul, leaving Stan alone.

Though he'd stopped thrashing, Paul held his hand just below the chest bandages. "It hurts, Rog," he gasped. Roger guessed from the pain in Paul's face that he wasn't just talking about the physical pain.

Monique calmly strode into the room as Roger took Paul's hand and held on. "Okay, Officer Tomlinson, I need you to take a few breaths like we did last time. Can you do that for me?"

Her calming voice stayed even, though Roger could clearly see her quickly assess the situation and move to the computer monitor.

Nodding, Paul attempted to comply but winced with each intake of air.

"I'm right here, sweetheart." Roger clutched his hand tighter. "Take in a deep breath."

Paul sucked in air as a tear slid down his cheek.

Bringing his other hand to Paul's face, he cupped his cheek and wiped away the tear with his thumb. "Now, let it out. Nice and slow."

With a shudder and a sob, Paul let out the breath. His eyes were still wide with fear, but his breathing slowly calmed with a few more breaths. He blinked his eyes as another tear escaped.

"That's it. I'm right here. Everything's okay." He kept

his palm pressed against Paul's cheek.

Monique injected a syringe of medication into the IV port. "This will help you calm down." She held Paul's gaze. "You doing better?"

"Yeah," he wheezed out. "Better. Thanks."

"That's a boy." She smiled at him. "Keep up that breathing. Oxygen is good for you." She patted his shoulder then looked at Roger. "You want me to send away the man standing outside?"

Roger shook his head before Paul could answer. "Could you have him wait for me on one of the chairs by the nurse's station?"

"Will do." She moved toward the door then shot another glance at Paul. "Now, you don't hesitate to call me if you need anything, okay, sugar?"

Paul nodded. "Thank you."

She stepped into the hallway.

Roger watched Stan converge on her through the open door.

"Okay, sir, if I could have you follow me to the waiting area…"

"Is Paulser all right?" Concern dripped from Stan's words.

"He'll be fine. Please come with me. Mr. Matthews will be right with you." Her footsteps and those of Paul's father receded down the hallway.

His heart finally calming, Roger let out a deep breath. "Are you okay, sweetheart?" He brushed his thumb along Paul's cheek bones.

With eyes glistening and red-rimmed, Paul looked up

at him. "Yeah, now that you're here."

"I'm sorry I didn't make it before he showed up." Roger glanced at the clock on the wall. "He was early."

"Yeah." Paul sniffled. "Damn it. I hate crying in front of other people."

"I'm not other people. You can bawl your eyes out as long as I get to hold you in my arms and comfort you." Roger kept stroking this thumb on Paul's cheek.

His lover's lip trembled. "I love you so much."

Roger leaned forward and molded his lips to Paul's. He felt Paul relax under him, and he pulled back, staring into his partner's eyes. "I love you, too." His hand slid down Paul's cheek and neck to rest on his shoulder. "Are you sure you're okay?"

"Yeah." Paul's eyes fluttered. "Whatever she put in the IV is making me sleepy."

"Then get a little rest, sweetheart. I'll be right outside."

Paul struggled to stay awake. "You're gonna talk to him?"

"Yeah. Do you want to try again another day?"

"No." Paul closed his eyes. "Never again." His breathing became more even as he slipped into slumber.

With a frown, Roger let go of Paul's hand and quietly stepped from the room, making sure to dim the lights and close the door. He strode down the hall and joined a miserable Stan Tomlinson in front of the nurse's station.

Monique called from the desk. "Does he need anything?"

Roger shook his head. "He's fallen asleep. Probably just needs some rest."

"That'll be good for him." She eyed Stan. "Sounds like he had a little too much stress."

Stan rose, but Roger cut off anything he was about to say. "Yes, but I'll make sure he doesn't have any more. If Paul needs me, I'll be in the cafeteria."

She nodded. "If something happens, I'll send someone down."

He turned to Paul's father. "Let's take a walk. Grab your coat." Roger bristled with annoyance at Stan Tomlinson. If he'd been in the room with the two men, he could have moderated the conversation.

Without a word, Stan glumly snatched the jacket from the chair and followed Roger down the hall toward the main elevator bank. While they waited, Roger turned to face him. "Doesn't sound like it went well."

"No, it didn't." Stan stared at his shoes. "He doesn't want me to come back, does he..." It definitely wasn't a question.

Roger sighed as the door opened. "That's what he said, but he's in a vulnerable state." They stepped inside with a few other people, so Roger cut off the conversation. The short elevator ride gave Roger a moment to collect his thoughts, reflecting on the pain and fear in Paul's eyes as he struggled with the anxiety attack, and the obvious disappointment the senior Tomlinson exhibited after the second rejection from his son.

Once they reached the level with the cafeteria, Roger led the way into the large open kitchen. They both got some coffee, and Roger paid for it. Heading away from the cashier, they found a table in a corner, away from the few other diners.

Roger took a sip of his coffee then addressed Stan. "I'm sorry you've come all this way to be rejected."

Stan shook his head. "I knew it was a risk, but I'd built it up to myself that I could convince Paulser to give me a chance to make things right."

"He may change his mind after he's released and has time to heal. I imagine being this vulnerable is something he hasn't had to deal with since he was out on the streets." Roger shifted uncomfortably in his seat. "Look, he only just told me about the selling himself thing a couple of days ago. I'd be obliged if you didn't tell anyone else about it, especially his mother."

"The whole family has no contact with me, but I'll keep it to myself." Stan sat with his elbows on the table and ran his hands over his face. "Just makes what I did worse."

Roger glanced up to see Tasheeka enter the cafeteria. She looked around and spied him. A frown formed on her face when she saw Stan, but she approached the table.

"Well? Did he forgive you?" With the now familiar head bobble and dripping attitude, she crossed her arms and pursed her lips. "Or did he tell you to go to hell?"

Lifting his head from his hands, Stan shot her a red-rimmed glare. "You'll be happy to know he doesn't want to see me again."

She puffed out a breath then pulled a chair up to the table and sat. "Look, Stanley. What you did destroyed our family, but I'm just as much to blame for not stopping you." With a heavy sigh, she patted her ex-husband's arm.

"I'm gonna talk to him for you."

Narrowing his eyes, he stared. "Why would you do that?"

"You're different now. I can see it. Melia could see it." She softened her stern expression. "You're more like you were thirty years ago when we were in college."

Roger shifted uncomfortably in his chair. With the quick change in tone of the conversation, he took a last gulp of his coffee. "Maybe I should leave you two to speak in private." Roger made to rise, but Tasheeka caught his arm in a firm grasp.

"No, don't you run away, Roger. You're part of the family, so you should know the bad with the good." She let go and patted the table. "Now, just sit back down, and we'll see if we can't work this out."

Stan's eyebrows rose in surprise. "Part of the family?"

"The boys are getting married." She gave a tentative grin to Roger. "I hope it was okay to tell him."

Roger shook his head. "I have no objection, but I wish it had been Paul."

In spite of his sadness, Stan smiled. "Well, congratulations." He looked away with a furrowed brow as if in thought for a moment and then turned back to Roger. "What do you need for your place? Can I do anything to…" His words trailed off, and he shook his head. "I'm sorry. Paulser probably wouldn't want anything from me."

Roger nodded. "Not now, but maybe we can give him some time."

Her expression thoughtful, Tasheeka stared at her ex-husband with disbelief in her eyes. "You're genuinely happy for them, aren't you?"

"I told you," Stan said as he met her gaze. "I've had a lot of time to think," he said, his deep voice trembling, and his eyes filling with tears. He brought his hands up, placing his wrists on the tabletop and clenching his hands. "I just want some contact with my family. I want to see my grandson, and I want to be a part of my children's lives."

She frowned. "And me?"

The expression of pain on the older man's face made Roger's heart ache. He couldn't believe he felt any sympathy for someone who'd hurt Paul, but seeing the man so full of remorse and regret changed his mind about Stanley Tomlinson. The man had learned his lesson and paid a high price for the education.

Stan dropped his gaze. "If you wanted to try a friendship, or at least some contact about our kids, I'd be willing. I didn't think you'd want anything to do with me."

"I don't want a damn thing to do with drunk and frustrated Stanley." She crossed her arms. "If you're still that way, forget it."

"I haven't had a drink in twelve years, and I'm still paying a therapist to help me grapple with my life." He looked into her eyes, earnest and contrite. "That Stan is gone. I swear I'm completely different now."

The couple's gazes locked for a long, poignant moment. Tasheeka relaxed her stiff posture, and Stan sat forward.

Roger felt like he was intruding on a very private and

intimate exchange between Paul's parents. "Look, I'm going back upstairs." He stood and pushed in the chair. "I have your number, Mr. Tomlinson, and I'll be in touch. If you want…" Roger hesitated, reluctant to offer something Paul wouldn't want. He pushed ahead anyway. "I can let you know how he's doing."

"I'd appreciate that." Stan's face held some hope behind the sorrow.

But that was as much as Roger could offer. He shook Stan's hand then gave a small wave to Tasheeka and left the cafeteria. Though Paul's interaction with his father had been nearly disastrous, Roger had been able to bridge a gap between Stan and his family. Now, if he could only convince Paul to afford the man the same chance to reconcile…

First things first, though. He needed to get Paul home and recuperated before any more big family interactions.

CHAPTER ELEVEN

THE SOCIAL WORKER stepped into the room as Roger and Melia sat with Paul on Monday morning, ten days after Paul's admission into Harborview. Tasheeka had returned to Tampa for work, and Melia's husband and little boy had gone with her. Melia stayed behind to spend some time with her brother, confident Pauley would be well taken care of.

"I'm Lisa Steiner. Dr. Sakurai had asked me to come in when your parents were first here, Officer Tomlinson." The woman's long, blonde hair lapped at her angular face as she strode to Paul's bed. "I'm sorry I wasn't available."

"No problem. We managed." Paul shrugged, a smile curving his mouth. "Call me Paul. When do I get sprung from this joint?"

Roger noted that Paul's gaze didn't match his easy smile. Despite his injuries, Paul was restless and more than a little grumpy with the speed of his recovery. The last thing he'd wanted to do was spend another weekend in the hospital, but Dr. Sakurai had thought he needed a couple more days to recuperate. Thankfully, she'd come in the prior evening and assured Paul he'd be going home. Jason rushed to offer a ride home from the hospital, and Roger had gratefully accepted.

She laughed. "Today for sure, Paul. I have the release orders processing, and we'll get you set up with both a physical and a respiratory therapist."

Paul billowed out a shaky breath. "So, I can go home? No rehab center?"

Ms. Steiner smiled. "Yes, you'll be heading home. I understand your partner will be looking after you." She glanced at Roger.

Roger nodded. "I'll keep him in line." Roger arched an eyebrow at Paul. It would be a long couple weeks if he started pushing himself.

Stepping into the room, Dr. Sakurai smiled brightly. "Hello, Paul. How are you feeling this morning?"

"Really good, Doc. I get to go home." Paul beamed, glancing at Roger. The mischievous gleam returned to his eyes.

Though excited to have Paul out of the hospital, Roger worried about the next part of the recovery. Therapy appointments followed by long stints alone in the house. Roger knew he couldn't take off too much more from work, and he didn't want to abuse Herrington's good will.

"I've signed off on the release paperwork, Lisa, so he should be good to go." Dr. Sakurai turned to Roger. "I'll have a list of instructions for you to help with his in-home care."

"Thanks," Roger said as he took Paul's hand. "I'm so grateful for everything you've done."

"All part of the friendly service." She nodded at Paul. "Take care of this brave man. I understand he got shot trying to help a woman being threatened and abused."

Paul blushed. "Just doing my job."

"Well, it was my honor to help you. Take care, Paul, and I wish you both well."

As the doctor departed, Lisa stepped back to the bed. "You'll need to sign some paperwork as well, Roger, but I expect Paul will be ready to go in about an hour." She followed Dr. Sakurai out of the room.

Melia stood and crossed to Paul. "I can stay a couple weeks to help out. Roger said something about a spare room. I can stay with you—unless you boys want your privacy."

Casting a quick glance at Paul who smiled, Roger nodded. "We'd be happy to have you. Thanks for the help. I was worried about leaving him alone."

"Why?" Paul huffed. "I can take care of myself."

Unfazed by his bluster, Roger crossed his arms. "I'm worried you'll try to escape from your confinement and go back to work. Or do something stupid like fixing the banister in the stairwell and overexerting yourself."

Paul cocked an eyebrow. "The banister needs fixing?"

With a roll of his eyes, Roger shook his head. "No, it was just an example."

Laughing, Melia looked from one to the other of them. "Are you sure you aren't married already?"

Monique knocked at the door. "Hi, Paul. I've come to release you from your IVs, sugar." She moved toward the bed.

"Thank goodness." Paul grinned at Roger. "It's really happening. I'm going home with you."

Roger patted his hand. His partner's excitement was contagious. "Yup, it's really happening."

Monique made short work of removing the IVs and bandaged the skin where the ports came out. "There you go. You take care of yourself, hear?"

"Yes, ma'am." Paul saluted her.

As she left the room, a middle-aged man in scrubs knocked and came through the door. "Hi, Officer Tomlinson. I'm John Powell, one of the physical therapists here at Harborview. Are you ready to get on your feet and try some more walking?"

Paul pushed away the sheet covering his legs. "More than. Let me try to get up on my own."

Standing back, Roger waited to see how Paul did but was ready to sprint forward and catch him if he started falling. Paul pushed up to sit. After a few moments, he dropped his feet to the floor and stood.

"Carefully, sweetheart." Roger moved next to him with John on the other side ready to catch him.

With a few shaky steps, Paul's stride became more confident as he navigated his way across the room and back. He puffed a bit but returned to the side of the bed and sat. "That was harder than I thought."

"You did great, and even got up by yourself. Better than any of the days this weekend," John said as he stepped to the monitor and logged in. "You'll need to walk as much as is comfortable each day." He swung his gaze away from the screen. "That does *not* mean doing anything strenuous for at least two more weeks."

Shifting his gaze between the physical therapist and

Roger, Paul frowned. "Have you two been talking to each other behind my back?"

Chuckling, John returned his attention the screen. "No, but if he gave you the same order, he'd make an excellent therapist."

Paul glanced at his sister, who raised one eyebrow. "If you think you'll get a break with me, you've got another thing coming."

With a shrug, Paul leveled his gaze on both Roger and Melia. "We'll see."

Roger sat next to him and slipped an arm across his back. "If you behave, I'll make it worth your while." He traced his fingers along the strong muscles of Paul's back.

With a head-bob reminiscent of their mother, Melia crossed her arms. "And I'll make sure you behave."

Paul huffed. "I know this tactic. I *am* a police officer, you know."

Finishing his typing, John logged off the computer and stepped toward the door. "But which of you is the bad cop?"

Roger turned to the therapist as he ran a finger up Paul's spine, getting the involuntary shiver he was hoping for. "Oh, that's definitely me."

"I'll behave," Paul promised.

Melia giggled. "I don't know, Paulser. Like our little Italian neighbor says, if you can't behave, be good."

They all laughed at that.

"It was a pleasure meeting you, Officer Tomlinson. I've left some notes and instructions that should print out with the discharge paperwork to take to your therapists."

He shook Paul's hand, and then Roger's and Melia's. "Take care of yourselves."

"Thanks, John." Roger pulled the cell from his pocket. "I let Jason know last night you were being released this morning, and he's coming to get us. I'll message him. By the time he gets here, we should be finished with the paperwork." He fired off a quick text and stood. "How about we get you dressed?"

"Sounds good." Paul glanced at his sister. "Mind standing guard at the door while I get naked with my man?"

"Don't worry, I'll make sure no one else stares at your hairy butt like I just had to." She left the room and closed the door.

Paul rolled his eyes. "Sisters."

With a laugh, Roger strode to the closet and pulled out the sweatpants and T-shirt he'd brought after seeing Clark at the pub. "It's not high fashion, but should be comfortable."

"Anything but this hospital gown." Pushing himself off the bed again, Paul steadied himself.

"Let me." Roger stepped forward, their lips close but not touching. With Paul upright, his muscular frame again standing tall and proud, Roger reveled in the urge to caress and kiss every inch of his towering masculinity. "I can't wait to get you home." His fingers traveled around Paul's torso and pulled the fabric forward, hitching it over Paul's shoulders and letting the garment fall to the floor.

His lover stood before him naked, and Roger knelt in front of him. "Oops, we dropped your gown."

"Rog." With his voice shaky, Paul shifted his weight.

Lifting his gaze as he ran his tongue over Paul's rapidly inflating cock, Roger wriggled his brows. "Yes, sweetheart?"

"I won't have the strength to keep standing if you do that here." The dressing over his wounds stood in stark contrast to his umber skin. Paul sighed. "But maybe when we get home."

With a quick kiss and swirl of his tongue over the head, Roger grabbed the discarded hospital gown and stood. "Sorry, I couldn't resist."

"Don't be. I'm sorry I asked you to stop." Paul brought his arms around Roger. "I'm excited to go home with you."

Roger kissed him tenderly, careful not to press against his bandages. "Let's get the shirt on first." Stepping back, he tossed the gown on the bed and retrieved the shirt and sweatpants.

With a wince, Paul managed to raise his arms straight out, and Roger slid the shirt onto his arms and over his head. Paul swayed and reached out, grabbing Roger's shoulder.

"Are you okay?" Roger's concerned gaze zeroed in on Paul.

"I'm good. Just got a little lightheaded for a second. Let's try the pants." Paul lifted a leg, one hand planted on the bed railing.

Roger sank to his knees again and pulled the sweats up one leg then the other. He rose, bringing the waistband over Paul's hips and butt. As he stood completely, he brought his arms around his lover.

With rap on the door, Melia poked her head in. "I better not be about to see a blow job going on."

"You wish," Paul shot back, winking at Roger.

"The social worker needs you to sign some paperwork, Roger. Can you meet her at the nurse's station?" She eyed her brother. "I'll stay here with Paulser."

Paul frowned. "Aw, I want to stay with the *good* cop."

Melia laughed as she lifted her buzzing cell from her pocket. She slid a finger across the screen and lifted the phone to her ear. "Hi, Mamma." She nodded at Paul. "Yeah, he's here. We're still at the hospital, but Roger's going to sign the paperwork, and we'll be taking the patient home."

Turning to his partner, Roger helped him sit back on the bed. "You talk to your mom, and I'll go take care of the paperwork."

Melia strode to the bed and handed over the phone.

"Hey, Mamma." He grinned at Roger. "She says hello."

"Tell her I say hi. I'll be back shortly." Roger left the room as Paul continued his conversation. He hurried to the nurse's station to find Lisa Steiner waiting for him.

"Hi, Roger. I've got the discharge papers here. I just need you to sign off that you'll be taking care of him. I also have instructions printed from the physical therapist and a phone number for the respiratory therapist. Make sure he makes an appointment as soon as possible to get started." She handed him a pen.

Roger read over the documents and signed, bursting

with excitement to be taking the last step to bring Paul home. "I'm glad we have a wheelchair. He's not ready for a long walk to the car."

Jason strode out of the elevator and spied Roger at the desk. "Hey, Roger. How's it looking? Ready to go?"

Handing Roger a copy of the paperwork in a blue folder, Lisa turned to Monique. "Let's get the wheelchair."

With a grin, Jason patted Roger on the shoulder. "You go back to the room and get Paul ready to go. I'll be there in a minute."

The twinkle in Jason's eyes gave Roger a moment's pause. "What's going on?"

"Nothing at all," Jason said, each word deliberate and slow.

Furrowing his brow, Roger eyed the officer decked out in his uniform. "Hmm."

"See you in a few minutes." Jason headed toward the restroom.

Roger exchanged a look with Lisa, who shrugged. Then he headed back to Paul's room.

"Okay, Mamma, Melia will call when we get to the condo." He rolled his eyes at Roger. "Okay, thanks for calling. Bye."

"We're waiting for the wheelchair, and then we'll be ready to go. Jason just got here." Roger sat next to him on the bed.

Monique pushed the wheelchair into the room a few moments later. "Ready to go, Paul?"

"Sure am."

Roger helped him stand and then sit in the chair. "You

okay?"

A grumpy frown creased Paul's lips. "I could have walked," he grumbled.

Melia crossed her arms. "Getting started on the difficult patient act so soon? You have to work up to walking long distances. You'd collapse before we got halfway down the hall. I'm not hauling your ass off the floor because you were too dumb to sit in a wheelchair."

"That's right, sugar." Monique nodded. "You just sit back and enjoy the ride."

Jason sauntered into the room, the same mischievous glint in his eyes. "Ready?"

CHAPTER TWELVE

"HOLY SHIT!" PAUL'S JAW dropped as a cheer went up in the hallway. Jason led the way like a band leader twirling a baton as Roger pushed Paul's chair down a column of at least twenty uniformed SPD officers flanking each side of the corridor. Fighting the swell of emotion, Roger turned to Melia, who was wiping away a tear from her eye.

As Jason pushed the wheelchair, the officers continued clapping and cheering, giving Paul a pat on the shoulder or an encouraging word as he passed. Roger recognized several of Paul's coworkers, who in turn shook his hand or grinned wildly. Paul's gaping jaw closed into a wide smile. He waved at the crowd of his friends and fellow officers.

Fred Collier stood next to Sarah Templeton at the end of the line of cops near the elevator with a pool cue. "Alex couldn't be here, but we're expecting you at the pub as soon as you get well enough. Mike's great and all, and we've won the first two rounds, but I want you to finish off the tournament with me."

"I'll do my best. Maybe my fiancé will take me in a couple weeks."

Fred's eyes sprang wide. "Your *what?*" His voice rose

in volume as a wide smile spread across his face. "You and Roger are getting hitched?"

Another cheer went up, and a second round of back slaps and hand shaking ensued. A half hour passed before the elevator doors closed on the four of them. Relief settled over Roger at the quiet.

Melia turned to her brother. "Wow, Paulser, you're definitely loved. I can't imagine my coworkers cheering like that for me if I were in the hospital."

"They're a great group." Paul craned his neck to look at Jason. "You arranged that?"

Jason gave a one-shouldered shrug. "Maybe."

Roger chuckled. "That's what your smug little smile was about when I was signing the discharge papers. I figured you were up to something."

"Thanks, buddy," Paul said as he faced forward again. "I was glad to go home, but it really lifts my spirits to see my friends."

Jason turned to Roger. "We're all willing and waiting to help. You can call on any of us."

"You're great, Jason." Paul sighed as he met Roger's eyes. "When can I play pool again?"

"Like you told Fred, how about we give it a couple weeks. At least until the physical and respiratory therapists clear you to exert yourself a little." Roger considered the movement of using a pool stick. "The motion of taking a shot at a rack of balls might be a little much for your chest."

The bell dinged, and the elevator doors opened. Jason pushed Paul's chair out and down the hallway to another set of elevators. The doors were already open, so they got inside and Jason pushed the P2 button. Once the doors closed, they descended into the parking garage.

Roger considered how he would manage to keep Paul occupied as he recovered at home. His partner was never one to just sit and read a book. He wasn't sure and had forgotten to ask how soon they could even make love, let alone get him out of the house to do any sort of physical activity.

Jason helped get Paul into the car then closed the door and turned to Roger. "Do you need any help when you get back to your place?"

"I think we'll manage. Just drop us off at the front. Thanks for everything. Getting his fellow officers together meant a lot." Roger reached out and hugged Jason.

"Glad to. He's an important part of the team." Jason stepped back and waved at Paul. "Really, let us know if you need anything. One of the guys will come by and help."

Paul pushed open the vehicle door. "What's going on out there?"

"Okay, okay." Roger turned back to Jason. "The patient isn't patient, apparently."

Jason laughed. "I was just reminding Roger to call if you need anything. Like being restrained to your bed." Jason nudged the door closed again before Paul could say anything further. He trotted around to the driver's side of the car as Roger slid into the back next to Melia. With a pat on Paul's shoulder, Roger sat back and buckled his belt. "Ready to go home?"

★　★　★

JASON DROPPED ROGER, MELIA, AND PAUL off at the condo, and Roger called the elevator in the front lobby of the building. The door opened. "All aboard," Roger said as he helped Paul into the waiting elevator.

They rode the car up and exited on the third floor. Keeping his arm firmly around Paul's waist, Roger helped him move along the hallway to the front door of the condo. "How're you doing, sweetheart?"

"Fine," Paul grunted. Though his breathing was a little labored, he pushed forward. Roger tried to support his weight as much as he could.

"Yeah, right." Melia followed with the bag of Paul's things. "You look like you're about to fall over."

"Thanks, Meli." Paul shot his sister a glare as he tried to straighten up and walk on his own.

Roger kept hold of his waist. "Don't get all macho on us, Paul. Right now, you're *supposed* to be tired."

Paul gritted his teeth but didn't let go of Roger.

They reached the door, and Roger turned to Paul. "Are you strong enough to stand on your own while I unlock the door?"

He nodded and leaned against the wall. As Roger pulled the keys from his pocket, he noted Paul's coloring was a bit pale, though not like he'd been when first in the hospital. Melia was right. He looked like he needed a good, long rest.

Roger pushed open the door and helped Paul into the condo. The tension Paul had been exuding dissipated as he stepped into his home. They moved into the kitchen, and

Roger helped him onto one of the chairs.

"Thanks, Rog."

Melia looked around. "Wow, Paulser, what a beautiful condo. You own this?"

With a grin, he nodded. "Well, I own about ten of the boards of the hardwood floor in the living room. The bank owns the rest."

She giggled. "We just bought a place in Tampa last year. I think we own less of our house than that."

"If you want to put that bag in the first bedroom on the right, I'll take care of it later." Roger led her into the hallway. "The bedroom on the left is all yours. Do you need any help getting your bags from the hotel?"

She shook her head as Roger handed her the car keys. "I can get them just fine. Thanks for loaning me your car." She carried the bag into the bedroom.

Returning to the kitchen, Roger retrieved a glass from the cabinet and filled it with water. He sat next to Paul and pushed the glass in front of him. "Let's keep you hydrated."

Paul regarded him with tired eyes. "Are you going to wet nurse me like this all the time?"

"I doubt you'll mind when I give you a bath." Roger winked. "Promise."

Lifting the glass to his lips, Paul grinned.

Chapter Thirteen

R OGER MARVELED AT the progress Paul made in the two weeks since his release from the hospital. The respiratory therapist gave Paul the okay to begin exercising again, which relieved Roger. Though he and Melia ensured compliance, Paul had been going stir crazy with cabin fever at not getting out more than a hour or so per day.

The bandages had come off a couple days before, and the wounds were held closed with stitches. Paul's regular doctor had been quite happy with his recovery. Roger had to keep reminding Paul not to scratch his chest, and thankfully, Paul was scheduled to have the stitches removed in another week.

They sat around the table the evening before Melia returned to Florida. Roger had cooked them roast beef and mashed potatoes with a beef gravy and broccoli. Melia poured herself another glass of red wine then filled Roger's glass. Paul hadn't really touched his.

"Thanks," Roger said as he raised a glass. "To family reunions."

"I'll drink to that," Melia said as she clinked his glass.

Paul picked at his food, deep in thought.

Arching an eyebrow, Roger glanced at his lover.

"Paul?"

He snapped his head up. "Huh?"

"I was toasting to family reunions." Roger set his glass back onto the table. "Something on your mind?"

Paul paused, and his eyebrows furrowed. "Melia and I talked about Dad." He stared at his sister. "Sorry, Meli. Not gonna happen."

Melia took a sip of her wine and slowly placed the goblet in front of her. "Paulser, he's different. I spent a couple days with him when you were first out of the hospital, and I could barely believe the change. He doesn't drink anymore, and he's full of regret over what happened."

"I regret it, too." Paul flashed her a glare. "I regret missing out on that scholarship at Tampa State. I regret missing out on my family for fifteen years. I regret sell..." He glanced at Roger. "*Doing* what I had to in order to survive on the streets."

"Paul," Roger warned, pushing as much concern as he could into his tone. "The last thing you need is an anxiety attack or a blood pressure spike." He knew Paul didn't want to share with his sister about the ways he survived the streets like he'd blurted out in anger at his father.

"Okay, okay." He waved his hands at Roger before returning them to the table. "I'm calm."

"Obviously," Roger snorted.

"Hey." She placed her hand over his. "This is my fault as much as Dad's. I should never have told you to come out to him."

"You couldn't have known," Paul said as he grasped

her hand. "I never thought he'd throw me out." He released his grip and stared at the food on his plate.

"Why did you give Mamma another chance?" Melia pressed. "She walked away from you when you needed her, and yet you forgave her."

"It's different," he grumbled.

"How?"

Fire flared in Paul's eyes again, and he brought his fist down on the table. "He called me a faggot and beat the hell out of me." The plates and silverware rattled, and Roger grabbed at their wine glasses to keep them from toppling over.

"Shit." Paul winced as he rubbed at his chest.

Roger frowned, concerned by Paul's outburst. He placed a hand on his partner's shoulder. "Calm down. If you're getting so upset about this, you haven't dealt with the emotions. Maybe we should look into a therapist."

"A shrink?" Paul shrieked. "Are you fucking kidding me?"

Roger hardened his voice and his stare. "Calm down."

Pushing back his chair, Paul stood and shook his head. "We're not discussing this again. That bastard can rot in hell." He turned on his heel and marched from the kitchen.

Melia sighed. "Sorry, Roger. I didn't mean to spoil your nice dinner."

Roger sat back. "Don't worry about it. He's going to have to deal with this eventually. After fifteen years of anger and hatred, I don't think he can fathom that the man he built up as a monster could be anything but."

"I suppose." She took another sip of her wine. "Did you talk to Dad at all?"

"A couple times. The last time was with your mother." Lowering his voice, Roger glanced out the door to the kitchen but didn't see Paul. "He asked me to send him updates on how Paul's doing, and I've been texting him."

Melia shrugged. "So have I." She made no attempt to lower her voice.

Roger jolted. "Really?"

"Yeah." She swirled the wine in her glass, watching the liquid come just to the lip of the goblet without spilling over. "He's different, and I'm giving him a second chance." She shrugged. "Who knows? He might fuck up again, but I doubt it. I've got the grandchild leverage over him now."

Paul carried a box into the kitchen and set it on the counter. "What's this, Roger? It's addressed to me but went to your office." He narrowed his eyes. "From Florida."

Meeting Paul's questioning gaze, Roger hoped his face didn't show too much guilt. "Open it and see." Though he had no idea of the contents, Stan had texted a week ago and asked if he could send something to Roger to give to Paul. Apparently, he was afraid Paul would toss it into the garbage unopened if he sent it directly to the condo. He chuckled to himself as he remember how Elsibeth had buzzed around the box, curious as to what was inside. He'd had a hard time dislodging it from her grip.

With a frown, Paul grabbed a pair of scissors from the junk drawer next to the dishwasher and ran the blade of one side of the shears along the seam. Popping the packing tape on the lid, he pushed back the paper and lifted out an old photo album.

Melia jumped to her feet. "That's Grandma Pauline's album. She was meticulous about labeling pictures. She must have given it to Dad before she died."

His brow furrowing, Paul turned the book over in his hand, examining the worn cover. "Why is he sending it to me?"

Roger stood and picked up his wine glass from the table. "Let's take it into the living room. The kitchen is too messy."

Waiting a moment after Paul and Melia left the room, Roger looked inside the box. There was a card partially hidden by the packing paper. He plucked the envelope from the box and strode into the living room.

The album lay open on the coffee table. Paul and Melia were bent over the book, examining a page.

Paul pointed to one of the pictures with reverence. "Grandma and Grandpap when they got married."

Melia shook her head. "He was such an old man when we were growing up. I remember sitting on his lap."

Paul chuckled. "I remember riding on his shoulders. They had that buzzer where the archway went from the living room into the kitchen. Grandma would buzz out to his workshop when she wanted him to come into the house or pick up the phone." He glanced up at Roger. "It also rang the doorbell in the house."

With a giggle, Melia returned her attention to the album. "You'd push it, and Grandma would come running out of the bedroom or the bathroom and open the front door to find no one outside." She turned to her brother, her voice pitched higher. "Paulser Tomlinson, you little stinkpot. Quit pushing that bell."

"And then I'd push it again and almost fall off Grandpap's shoulders, because he'd start laughing." Paul's smile faded somewhat when he turned the page. "Mamma and Dad's wedding day."

Melia sighed. "I can't believe she was ever that skinny."

"Dad had a full head of hair." Paul ran a finger over the photograph then turned the page again.

After a sip of wine, Roger moved to the couch and sat down next to Paul, setting the card in his lap and wrapping an arm around his partner's back. He stared at the next photo. It was a very young-looking Stan and Tasheeka Tomlinson with two small children. They were all laughing for the photographer.

"Do you remember that day, Meli?" Paul asked with a tremble in his voice.

"Yeah," she nodded. "That's when Grandma took us all to the county fair after Grandpap died."

"You and I got cotton candy and pushed it into each other's faces. Dad had to help me get it off my face and out of my nose." Paul trailed off, seeming to lose himself in thought.

Melia turned another page. A thirteen-year-old Paul was swinging a baseball bat. The five-by-seven picture had been snapped just as the bat connected with the ball. In the background, a younger Stan Tomlinson had his fists in the air, his mouth open in a proud cheer. The opposing page held two smaller pictures, one of Paul standing butt to butt and head to head with his father. A ruler perched on the tops of their heads. Roger could see the mischief on Stan's face as he squatted a bit to make Paul believe they were the same height. The caption under the picture was scrawled in the neat handwriting of the entire album: *The bigger man.*

The other picture was clearly not the original picture to occupy the space. The corner edges were newer, holding a picture of Stan quite a bit older than in the prior photo. He sat alone, his face worn and tired on an old porch swing dressed in a suit. The date underneath was five years ago, and the caption, in the same hand, though more shaky in its letter formation, read *The lesser man.*

Melia gasped. "That's the day I got married. He asked to come, but Mamma told him no. I didn't want him there either."

"Didn't Grandma come to the wedding?" Paul asked.

"Yes, she was there. She sat next to Mamma in the front row." Melia stared at the picture of their father. "She kept saying throughout the reception that you should have been there."

Paul's body shook a little as he closed his eyes.

Roger hugged him tightly and lay his head on Paul's shoulder, hoping to ease some of the pain his lover exuded.

Melia took Paul's hand. "She never forgave Dad. I'm surprised she even had this picture. I was under the impression she refused to see him after Mamma told her what had happened."

Opening his eyes, Paul turned to his sister. "Then how did he get the album?"

Roger let go of Paul and lifted the sealed envelope. "This was in the bottom of the box."

Paul stared at him for a moment then took the card. He pried the envelope open with a finger and lifted out a card. Inside, a photo and a handwritten letter slid out and nearly fell to the floor before Paul caught them.

The card had a photo of the beach at Tampa on the front, with the words *Wish You Were Here* in block letters across the top. Paul examined the photo. A woman Roger could only surmise as Paul's grandmother held a grinning toddler.

"Wow," Melia smiled. "It's you and Grandma."

Paul passed the picture to his sister as he unfolded the letter. Clearing his throat, he began to read out loud.

"My Dearest Paulser,

I still struggle to believe you are not part of our lives, and that your father could have done such a stupid and cruel thing to you. Though it grieves me to be separated from my own son and only child, I can never forgive his actions forcing you away from us.

If you are reading this, I've died and not gotten the chance to see you again. I'm no longer young, and I know my remaining time is short. It has been twelve years since I last saw you, and I had a hunch then you had something you wanted to tell me but didn't.

I want you to know that I love you no matter who you are or who is lucky enough to have earned your love and affections. I was fortunate to have met

*your grandpap and cherished every day we had to-
gether. I hope you have found someone who is worthy
of the exceptional man I know you are.*

*This album contains memories of our family and
our time together. There are blank pages in the back
to add pictures of your own family and treasured
moments. I hope your father has taken the opportunity to find you and give this to you. My lawyers have
instructions to deliver it to him upon my death.
Inside the card, there is the address and phone number for my attorneys. I've left the bulk of my financial
assets to you, including investments and cash. It is
held in trust until such time as you wish to claim it. I
am confident Melia will do well with the fine young
man she married, so I want to make sure you are well
taken care of should you find your way back to our
family."*

Choking back a sob, Paul raised emotion-filled eyes to
stare at his sister. "Did you know about this?"

Melia shook her head. "She left me a little bit of money, but I never knew if she'd done the same for you."

Roger took the letter from Paul's shaking hands. "Do
you want me to finish reading it?"

He nodded. "Thanks."

*"Though I can never forgive your father, I am re-
minded as I look through this album that there were
happy moments in our family. Perhaps time and
distance will allow you to remember these times, and
the two of you can find some sort of reconciliation. I*

remember my son before the drinking, and he was a kind and generous man. Maybe one day, he can be again.

I wish you every happiness and think of you each day. Be happy in your life, Paulser. You deserve only wonderful things.

My love,
Grandma Pauline"

Roger set the letter on the coffee table and opened his arms to Paul, who rested his forehead on Roger's shoulder. Enveloping his lover in an embrace, Roger kissed his neck and held on tight as a series of heavy sighs shook Paul's body.

After a few moments, Paul pushed himself up and sniffled hard. His eyes were red-rimmed and moist. "Okay. I give. I'll call him. You got his number, Meli?"

"Uh," Roger cleared his throat. "I already have it."

"Oh." Paul eyed him. "From the hospital, right?"

"Yeah, I've been giving him updates on how you're doing." Roger picked up his wine glass and took a sip, not meeting Paul's gaze.

"You have?" By his tone, Paul was surprised but not angered.

"He asked me to. I didn't tell you because I assumed you'd tell me to stop." Roger stared at the album. "He'd said that his mother disowned him, but I didn't know about the letter or your inheritance."

Melia crossed her arms. "Well, I've been doing the same thing, and I'm *not* sorry about it."

Paul's eyes widened. "You, too?"

"Yup."

Roger suppressed a small smile because the head bob she gave her brother completely matched the one their mother had given their father.

Paul stared back and forth at the two of them. "And what does he say?"

Melia shrugged. "He's grateful. The same for you, Roger?"

"Yeah," Roger said and drained the rest of the wine from the glass. Guilt burned in him for not telling Paul about the communications with Stan Tomlinson. The letter from Paul's grandmother confirmed that he'd done the right thing, though.

With a heavy sigh, Paul lifted Roger's chin to bring their gazes together. "It's okay. Don't feel bad."

Offering a weak smile, Roger nodded. "Thanks. I hated keeping it from you."

They spent another hour looking at the pictures in the album. Roger moved to one of the chairs after filling their wine glasses again and watched brother and sister laughing and crying at the memories in the book. He learned a lot about his lover's childhood and made a mental note to show Paul some of the albums his parents had.

As the evening got late, Paul carefully stretched and yawned. "I'm beat. You all ready to hit the hay?"

Melia nodded. "Are you still okay to get me to the airport in the morning, Roger?"

"No problem at all." He stood and gave her a hug. "See you in the morning."

Paul stood, closing the album and turning to his sister.

"Good night, sis." He hugged her. "I'm glad you stayed."

"Me, too." She stepped back after they'd embraced. "Make sure you call Dad. This has gone on long enough."

"Okay," Paul huffed. "I will."

Chapter Fourteen

ROGER STEPPED INTO the office then halted as Elsibeth rushed around the desk and flung her arms around him.

"Roger! It's so good to see you," she bubbled, a huge grin on her face instead of her patented scowl. "How is Paul? It's been at least a week since you've been in."

"He's doing well. The PT has cleared him to go back to work on light duty, and I'm really glad to get him out of the condo." He moved to the check-in board and wiped away the *on leave* next to his name. "How has Clark been doing?"

Her grin turned to a smirk. "He's amazing. I've never seen Marsha so smitten. In fact, he's managed to make a great impression with pretty much everyone here."

A frown tugged at Roger's lips. "Did Herrington offer him my job?"

"Absolutely not," his boss's voice boomed down the hall. "Clark does excellent work, but you're the controller here and don't you forget it." The older man winked at Elsibeth. "Besides, he turned down the job I offered him."

Roger crossed his arms and shook his head. "I knew it. Turn my back for a week, and he tries to edge me out of my office. I'm going to have a word with Mr. Adamson."

Herrington laughed. "Now, now. You know I didn't offer him *your* job." He clasped a hand onto Roger's shoulder. "If you'll excuse us, Elsibeth. I need to get this youngster reacquainted with the big project he's supposed to be shepherding."

"Absolutely, sir." She moved back around the counter and sat at her desk. "You have a ten-thirty appointment with the software developers. They called to say traffic was merciful, so they can be here as early as ten."

"Does that work for you, Roger?" Herrington checked his watch. "Should give you an hour to get settled, check your e-mail, then meet with me before they arrive."

Roger nodded. "Sounds great, Mr. Herrington."

As they set off down the hall, Elsibeth called out, "I almost forgot, Roger. There's a delivery for you on your desk." She raised an eyebrow. "And you never did tell me what was in that package."

"Thanks," he said as they continued down the hall. "You're right, I didn't," he called back to her.

With a chuckle, Herrington turned into his office. "See you in an hour."

Roger continued to his door and stopped at the entrance. On his desk perched a bouquet of two dozen red roses. Heat flushed through his face as he approached the flowers and lifted the small card from the plastic fork.

You're everything to me. Have a great day at work.

Love, Paul

"They're beautiful."

Roger jerked because he hadn't seen Angelica approach.

She grinned widely. "Everything good with your guy?"

"He's back to work today, and his recovery is proceeding better than the doctors expected."

"That's wonderful. I'll let you get to it. You probably have a big day ahead."

"Yup. The developers are coming."

"Good luck with the e-mail." She wriggled her eyebrows. "Just delete the ones from Marsha."

Roger laughed. "You got it."

She continued down the hallway as Roger sat at his desk and powered up his desktop. Rubbing his hands together, he clicked open his e-mail. "Here we go."

CLARK SHOWED UP at Roger's office after lunch. "Hey, buddy. How's the day going?"

Roger grinned up at him from his desk. "Great. I can't thank you enough for all the help while Paul was injured."

With a shrug, Clark sauntered in and sat in the chair opposite Roger. "Like I told you, this is friendship. You don't owe me a thing."

"Well, at least let me invite you over for dinner."

Clark grinned. "Now *that* I'll happily accept. The pub is great and all, but I don't need all the fried food." He nodded at the paperwork on Roger's desk. "Whatcha working on?"

"Final arrangements for the implementation. I think we're ready to sign the contract and install the software."

He eyed his friend. "Are you here to work, or is there something on your mind?"

"A little of both." He sighed. "I'm trying to steel myself to accept the invitation to dinner at my sister's soon-to-be in-laws. From the sound of it, they're worse than her boyfriend."

"Well, at least you know where he gets it." Roger smirked. "How about you take a date?"

Laughing, Clark shook his head. "Don't think so. Mitch is only available for the weekend in Anacortes."

His eyes wide, Roger stared hard at Clark. "Who's Mitch?"

Clark froze as some of the color drained from his face. "Oh, uh…I met Mitch online."

"You're taking an internet hookup to your sister's wedding?" Roger laughed and shook his head. "How long have you known this guy?" This didn't sound like Clark at all. The last Roger had heard, Clark had sworn off anything other than quick hookups after a series of disastrous dates.

"A few weeks. He's a nice guy." Clark looked distinctly uncomfortable, fidgeting in his chair.

Roger narrowed his eyes. "What's going on?"

"I'll tell you another time." He clapped his hands together. "So, I got Herrington a job description for what I think you need in an assistant. He said you were going to hire someone."

Reluctant to change the subject, Roger gave Clark a final inquisitive stare. "You're evading the question."

He gave a single nod. "Damned right, I am."

Seeing his friend was not going to reveal anymore, he relented. "Okay. Yeah, I finally got authorization to get some permanent help. It just got delayed because of Paul's hospital stay."

"I'll log in and e-mail you the document. Herrington approved it to send out, but I wanted you to see it just in case I missed something." Clark jumped up and hurried toward the office door.

"Clark," Roger called before he could leave the office. "You know you can tell me anything, right? I'm not going to judge you." He leaned forward. "Does this Mitch guy have a tiny dick or something?"

Clark burst out laughing. "No, no. It's plenty big. Don't worry about it, Roger. I'm good. I swear, I'll tell you about Mitch after the wedding."

"Okay. I'll let it go for now. Send me the job description, and we'll get it posted today."

With another nod, Clark fled out the door before Roger could say anything further. He returned his attention to his e-mail and plowed through several messages from Marsha. Angelica was right. He should have just deleted them. They were all variations on the same theme, mostly questions he'd already answered in the specs he'd sent out weeks ago.

The e-mail from Clark came through, and he read over the job description. Pretty standard stuff, and it all looked good—until he got to the final line of the required skills. *Exceptional oral skills and ability to crouch for long periods—be prepared to demonstrate proficiency at time of interview.*

Roger picked up his phone and sent a text to Clark.

A few moments later, Clark stood at the door with a

smirk on his face. "So, do you think the job posting is ready to send out?"

Shaking his head, Roger glared at his friend. "You're a shit sometimes. You know that, right?"

"Well, if you remember from our college days, I'm quite proficient in that skill. Good to know you read all the way to the bottom." Clark chuckled.

"And if *you* remember from our college days, I always get the bottom."

Clark roared out a laugh. "You sure did, though I'd wager that hunky cop of yours can get you to flip."

With a sigh, Roger shook his head again. "I can't believe you're having this conversation with me at work."

Shrugging, Clark stepped into the office. "It's not my workplace. I'm just filling in. Good thing you're HR."

"Oh, for goodness sake."

AT THE END of the day, Roger powered down his computer and pushed aside the small stack of paper from the center of his desk.

Herrington poked his head into the room. "Nice work today, Roger."

"Thanks. I'm glad to finally get the contract signed. We'll start the conversion next week."

His boss crossed his arms and leaned against the doorframe. "And Clark?"

Frowning, Roger sighed. "He has a large project starting up, so today was his last day helping out. I'll have to figure out some sort of thank you for everything he did."

The prospect of handling the actual implementation on his own didn't make him excited to come into work. Still, everyone had rallied around him when Paul was in the hospital, even Marsha. And, the light of the promised raise looked really good at the end of the tunnel.

Herrington smiled. "Well, I'm sure we can find some money in the budget to express our gratitude." He nodded at the flowers on Roger's desk. "Where did those come from?"

Roger warmed, looking at the roses. "Paul."

"Ah. Very sweet. Well, I've got some meetings in the early morning, so I'll see you around noon. Don't hurry coming in tomorrow. You did plenty today, and it's nearly six o'clock."

"Thanks. I'll see what Paul's schedule is and plan accordingly."

With a nod, Herrington strode away.

As Roger stood, his cell rang. Lifting the phone from his pocket, he was happy to see Paul's grinning face on the screen. "Hey, sweetheart."

"Hey, babe. I'm in the load zone outside. You finished for the day?"

Relieved to be saved the walk to the bus and the jostling around on the full express, Roger gathered the collection of sticky notes he'd written out during the day and placed them next to his office phone. "I just shut down and was thinking about a bus, but I'm happy to ride home with you."

"Dinner?"

He grabbed his coat from the rack and shut off the

light. "What did you have in mind?"

"Fred needs me to play pool. What do you think?"

Roger paused at the board in the reception area and furrowed his brow. "Are you sure you're ready for that? I know the PT said things were going well, but shooting a cue stick is a movement that might bother your chest."

"Let's give it a try. I'm dying to play. You'll get a pint and a meat pie out of it."

With his stomach rumbling, Roger moved the marker next to his name to OUT and strode out of the office. "And tater tots?"

Paul laughed. "Yeah, and tater tots."

"I'm just catching the elevator now." The doors opened, and Roger stepped inside. "Be there in about five minutes."

"Okay." The phone beeped twice as the call ended.

Pocketing the cell, Roger tried to clear his mind as he stood in the otherwise empty elevator, descending through the building. Once the door opened, he strode through the lobby of the building, noting Merrick was not at the podium, and headed out to the waiting truck.

"Not in the squad car today?" Roger asked as he pulled the door closed.

Paul rolled his eyes. "Nope. Desk duty," He grumbled then leaned over and planted a hard kiss on Roger's lips. Putting the truck in gear, he turned back to the road and pulled out into traffic.

"How did it go today?"

Keeping his gaze fixed on the pedestrians crossing Fourth Avenue as they waited to turn, Paul shrugged. "It was a day. I don't like being a desk jockey, but the PT said a month and I'm back on my beat."

"I don't mind you being behind a desk for a while." Roger caressed Paul's leg. "It means I don't have to worry about another phone call saying you've been shot."

Paul maneuvered the truck through the intersection and headed toward the Express Lane ramp. "You won't have to worry about that," he said, shooting him a quick look, one eyebrow raised. "I'm gonna be extra careful now that I'm getting married."

"You'd better be."

They drove along Interstate Five, and Roger enjoyed watching the lights of the University District pass by. Paul exited at Sixty-Fifth and pulled up to the pub a few minutes later. He shifted the truck into park and turned off the engine.

"We're here." He turned to Roger. "Seriously. I'll stay safe. I never want you to go through that again."

"I'm not a fan of the hospital part, but I like taking care of you." Roger brought his hand to Paul's face. "I love you, Paul."

"I love you, too, Rog." He leaned in, and they sealed their lips together in a tender kiss. The intensity increased, and Paul brought his arms around Roger to pull him in closer.

A rap on the window broke their kiss.

Grinning, Fred, Mike, and Jason stood at the driver's window.

Paul turned the key in the ignition and rolled down the window.

"Geez, guys. I might have to bust you for indecent exposure here in a minute," Fred crowed.

Jason laughed. "Ah, knock it off, Fred. We could charge admission."

Leaning in to Paul's ear, Roger whispered. "I know how you like to be watched."

"Uh, okay." Paul pushed open the door, making the three men jump back. "Let's go shoot some pool. This is getting out of hand."

"Why?" Jason leered. "Did Roger let go of your stick or something?"

They all laughed as Paul rolled up the window and pulled the keys from the ignition. After locking the truck, the five men strode into the pub. A cheer went up from several of the tables as Roger recognized quite a few of the officers from Paul's division with their various spouses and partners.

Alex Templeton stepped forward. "Hey, Paul. Glad you're here. We're facing off with the guys from the Northside Precinct." He looked expectantly at Mike. "Sarah can't be here tonight. She wasn't feeling well. You won't mind stepping in to play will you?"

Mike sighed dramatically. "I suppose." He eyed Fred, Alex, and Paul. "Do the four of you take turns not being here just to get me to wipe the table with the other unsuspecting officers?"

Chuckling, Roger noted the guilty expressions on Fred and Alex's faces. "I think that's exactly what's going on here."

Paul raised an eyebrow. "Seriously?"

Mike shot Roger a sly wink. "Maybe Jason should take Sarah's place since he's actually a *police* officer, and this is a *police* officer's tournament. Roger and I can just watch the blood bath."

Puffing out his chest, Jason furrowed his brow. "What? You don't think I can hold my own?"

Fred's eyes widened. "Are you kidding? You barely know which end of the stick is supposed to hit the cue ball."

The men laughed as Jason stood indignant. "I'll show you how it's done." He marched over to the table and grabbed a stick.

The rest of the men followed him over as he lined up a shot with the rubber end of the stick aimed at the eight-ball.

Fred shook his head. "What the hell are you doing, Lynch?"

Jason looked up, false innocence covering his face. "What?"

They all laughed again, including Jason. He handed the cue to Mike. "Here you go, baby. Clean their clocks."

Fred, Paul, Mike, and Alex settled into their game with four officers from the opposing precinct. Mike broke first and got three balls in. He turned to Jason and blew him a kiss. Roger marveled at the poetry of motion Mike's shots were. He sank four more balls and lined up the final shot for the eight ball. The four cops from the other precinct stood gaping as Mike called the corner pocket and thrust his stick to connect with the cue ball. It struck the eight, which perfectly hit two bumpers and rolled into the corner pocket. Mike blew on the end of his cue stick.

Paul's precinct cheered as the other officers just stared at each other. Jason slung a beefy arm over Roger's shoulder. "Come on, let's order some beers for the pool sharks."

They made their way around the tables of laughing and chatting patrons to a couple stools at the end of the bar.

Seb slid a beer across to a woman three stools down from the guys and hurried over to them. "Great to see you, Roger. What's your poison?"

"I'll do a Bodi, and Paul will have an IPA." He turned to Jason. "How about you?" Reaching into his pocket, Roger slipped his credit card out of his wallet.

"Mike will take a ginger beer. Let's get Fred a Fat Tire, and I'll do a Hefeweizen."

As Jason pulled out his wallet, Roger handed Seb his credit card. "Put it all on my tab. That includes all their food when we order."

Jason's brow furrowed as he looked from Seb to Roger. "Are you sure?"

"My raise will be really good." Roger shrugged. "I'm celebrating Paul getting back into normal life."

A cheer went up behind them. Expecting to see Mike running the table, Roger turned to find Paul, his arms raised in triumph, with Fred and Mike patting him on the back, and Alex beaming.

Roger locked eyes with his lover, and they both smiled. Paul pushed away from the group and trotted over to the bar.

"Did you win?" Jason stood and offered Paul his seat.

Paul grinned. "Sure did. Mike didn't even have to run the table. Those Northside guys are gonna be crying in their beers tonight."

Seb brought the drinks and set them down on the bar. "Here you go, guys. Yours is on the house, Paul. Glad to see you back in the saddle."

Paul lifted his beer in a toast. "All thanks to Roger."

Warmth filled Roger's cheeks.

Seb smiled. "Well, then, Roger's is on the house, too. Cheers, guys."

Roger turned to Paul. "He's getting a great tip."

Jason grabbed Mike's and Fred's pints. "Be right back."

"See what Alex wants," Roger called.

Nodding, Jason headed toward the pool tables.

"You and Jason doing okay?" Paul asked and took a sip of the beer.

"Just fine. I managed to get my credit card out faster." Roger smirked. "I'm buying for the team tonight."

"You sure, babe?"

"Yeah, I'm sure." He leaned in. "Let me know if you get too tired to stay, okay? You worked all day, and I don't want you to overdo it."

Paul cocked his head. "What's in it for me?"

"Well," Roger drew out the word as he leaned forward. "When we get home, I'll help you with your breathing exercises and your stamina training." He licked his lips and glanced at Paul's crotch.

Swallowing hard, Paul sat back and spread his legs.

"I'm getting very tired all of a sudden."

His seductive pose and leering gaze tried Roger's resolve.

"Now, now. It would be rude to run out on your teammates. Besides, you promised me tater tots." Roger waggled his finger. "Priorities."

Paul groaned. "Tease."

"Paul!"

They turned to see Fred waving him over.

"Gotta go, babe. Hold that thought." He stood. "Order me a couple meat pies?"

"You got it, sweetheart." Roger swatted his butt. "Get over there and win big for me."

Chuckling, Paul grabbed Jason's beer and hurried over to the pool tables.

With the bustle of the bar swirling around him, Roger took a moment to look around. Paul had a huge smile on his face as he passed the beer to Jason. His colleagues were cheering him on as he took the pool cue from Fred and leaned over, the curve of his butt jutting back as he lined up his shot. Jason had his arm around Mike's waist as they both sipped their drinks and watched the game.

Roger reflected over the last month. Feuding with Jason, Paul getting shot, the rollercoaster with Tasheeka and Stan Tomlinson, and getting engaged. He took a sip of his beer and smiled as another cheer went up around Paul. His lover still hadn't fulfilled his promise to his sister to call his father, but otherwise, things were finally going well.

Seb returned. "You guys ordering food?"

"Yup." Roger grabbed one of the menus and ordered for himself and Paul, and asked for Jason and Mike's usual.

Writing down the order, Seb glanced at Roger. "And a pile of tater tots?"

Roger grinned. "Definitely."

EPILOGUE

T HE BRIGHT FLORIDA SUN shone on the plain white siding of Paul's childhood home. Roger had expected a more interesting house, maybe stucco or a large stately home. Instead, the house was a modest white rambler with green trim. A neat lawn and groomed shrubs surrounded the structure, and a palm tree rose from a small patch of Bird of Paradise flowers a few feet from the sidewalk.

Paul took Roger's hand as they strode up the path to the two cement steps in front of the door. "This, babe, is where the road to you started. The last time I saw this house I had blood pouring out of my nose and scratches on my leg."

Roger squeezed his hand. "How are you doing?"

"I'm okay. The house is smaller than I remember. Childhood memory exaggerates perception." Paul's jaw clenched.

"Profound," Roger said as he pulled Paul to a halt. He pulled his lover into a hug. "This is going to be great."

"I hope so," Paul grumbled. "But we should've gotten a hotel."

Giving him an extra squeeze, Roger shook his head. "Your dad was very insistent we stay here."

The front door opened, and Stan stood at the threshold in a pair of khaki shorts and a deep blue T-shirt. With a chuckle, he waved. "Giving the neighbors a show?"

Stiffening, Paul pulled away, addressing his dad. "They're lucky they get it for free."

Laughing heartily, Stan came down the steps and stood before his son. He clasped a hand on his shoulder. "I'm so glad you're here."

With a nod, Paul let his dad pull him into an embrace.

"Mmm-mmm, Roger, you do look good in those shorts."

Roger spun around to meet Tasheeka's appraising gaze as she sauntered down the steps with a smirk. She looked relaxed and happy in a yellow sundress.

Paul broke away from Stan. "Mamma?"

"Hi, baby." She reached Roger and enveloped him in a hug. "How was the flight?"

Roger hugged her back then moved aside as her equally confused son embraced her. "Uh, it was good. We had a slight delay at Atlanta, but it worked out fine."

"What are you doing here, Mamma? I didn't expect to see you for a couple of days." Paul stood staring between his parents, who had moved to stand together. He narrowed his eyes. "What's going on here?"

"Well, baby," his mother started. "Your father and I are getting reacquainted. He invited me over."

"Uh, huh." Paul stood next to Roger, his brow furrowed.

"Melia will be over in a couple hours, but let's get you settled in your old room." Tasheeka nodded at the car.

"Do you have any bags?"

"I'll get them." Roger hurried to the trunk of the rental car and popped the hood as Paul's parents led him into the house. Something strange was going on between Stan and Tasheeka. They seemed far friendlier with each other than they were when she'd ripped into him at the hospital. Granted, they hadn't seen each other in fifteen years, but still.

Shouldering his backpack and grabbing Paul's case, he closed the trunk and trotted up the path to the house. As he entered, he followed the voices through the modest living room, down the short hallway lined with family pictures, and stopped at the entrance to the third door on the right. The bedroom smacked of a teenage boy, complete with science-fiction movie posters, plastic model battleships, a collection of superhero action figures on a glass shelf over a small wooden desk, and a small bust of Shakespeare perched on the windowsill. A framed picture of Paul, likely his senior picture, sat in the middle of the desk, like it was a placeholder until he returned.

Paul sat on the double bed with a parent on each side, staring at the floor. Tasheeka slung an arm around his waist and pulled him close. Stan patted his leg.

Roger stared at the trio. "Is everything all right?"

"Yeah, Rog. We're okay." Paul sniffled then stood and stepped across the small room. "Welcome to my childhood room."

Tasheeka stood. "Come on, Stanley. Let's leave these boys to get settled."

As Stan got to his feet, Tasheeka took his hand and led

him from the room. Paul stared after them as the door shut.

"This is how my room looked when I left, except it had piles of dirty clothes all over the place. The bed was rarely made, too." Still staring at the door, Paul shook his head. "He didn't throw anything away. Didn't try to erase me from the family." Moving to the closet, he opened the door and ran his hand along the neatly hung shirts and pants. "Even my clothes."

Roger came up behind him and slipped his arms around Paul's torso, lacing his fingers together. "Are you glad we came?"

"Yeah." He leaned back against Roger. "It's like I've been away forever but never left."

"So," Roger gave him a squeeze. "How many boys did you fuck on that bed?"

Bursting out laughing, Paul spun in his arms to face him. "No one on the bed."

Roger didn't miss the evasion. "But?"

"I bent Ryan Parks over the desk and fucked him." Paul smirked. "And at the window."

Chuckling, Roger leaned forward and kissed Paul's neck. "I knew you liked to be watched."

Paul checked out the open window, like he was envisioning he and Ryan going at it and looking for prying eyes. "No one saw."

"As far as you know." Roger noted the growing bulge in his lover's shorts. Sliding his hands downward, he cupped Paul's ass and pulled him closer. "When your parents are at work tomorrow, you're going to fuck the hell out of me on that bed."

A small gasp escaped Paul's lips.

"And then," Roger continued, his own cock tenting the front of his shorts. "On the desk."

"Fuck, babe—"

Roger pressed a finger to Paul's lips. "And *then* at the windowsill with the curtains open. I'll be the judge of how well hidden we are by the backyard fence."

Crushing their lips together, Paul picked Roger up and carried him to the bed. He lowered Roger onto his back, not breaking their kiss, and ground their bodies together. The warmth and friction made Roger's already stiff cock ache for release from his clothes. As Paul propped himself up on his arms, Roger stared up into his hungry eyes.

"I want you now, Rog." Paul thrust his hips forward, the hardness trapped in his shorts pressed firmly against Roger's own straining dick. The bed gave a loud squeak.

Roger lay his hand on Paul's chest, trying to show as much restraint as possible but wrestling with his conscience. "We really should join your parents in the living room."

With a groan, Paul rolled onto his back. "I guess. Tease."

A rap at the door had them both sitting up quickly, trying to hide their erections.

The door opened, and Tasheeka popped her head in. "Baby, we're gonna take a quick trip to the grocery store. I forgot a few things for dinner tonight. We'll see you in about an hour." She winked at them and closed the door.

Roger turned to Paul with an incredulous grin, and the

two of them burst out laughing.

AFTER DINNER, ROGER AND PAUL washed up the dishes in the kitchen as Stan and Tasheeka sat in the living room with Melia and her family. Roger leaned in and lowered his voice. "I'm glad I got to be the first person you fucked in your childhood bed."

Paul chuckled. "You'll be the only one who gets that honor." He placed a quick kiss on Roger's lips. "And tonight, you'll be the only one who gets to do the same to me."

Warmth flushed through Roger's skin. "Not the bed. The desk."

A pattering of little feet had them resuming their task at the sink. "Uncle Paul?"

Turning, Paul grinned at his nephew. "Yeah, buddy?"

"Are you moving in?" Little Pauley's face looked hopeful.

"No, but your mom is going to let you come to Seattle this summer. You want to come visit me and Uncle Roger?"

"Yeah!" He jumped up and down a few times then scurried from the kitchen.

Paul turned back to the dishes. "He's got a lot of personality."

Roger handed him a plate to rinse. "Just like his uncle." Ducking as Paul flicked water at him, Roger laughed.

They finished the dishes and joined the family, taking a seat on the couch. Pauley and Stan played with a pile of

LEGOs, while the rest of them sat in various chairs.

Stan patted Pauley on the head then crawled over to crouch next to Tasheeka. "Kids, we have something to tell you." He took her hand.

Paul and his sister exchanged a startled glance. Roger smiled as he realized why Tasheeka had been here when they'd arrived.

Placing her other hand on top of Stan's, Tasheeka smiled. "We've decided to get married again."

"What?" Paul and Melia squawked in unison.

"We've had plenty of time to talk through things since you were in the hospital, Paulser. I told you this family was broken. You weren't the only one missing." Tasheeka looked into her former husband's smiling face. "The alcohol is no longer an issue."

"And it never will be again," Stan interjected, turning to Paul. "I promise."

"Thanks, Dad," Paul acknowledged. "I appreciate that."

Tasheeka shifted her gaze to stare intently at Roger. "We all wouldn't be sitting here if it weren't for you. Thank you for calling and putting all this in motion."

Heat burned through Roger's cheeks as he met her gaze. Paul reached behind him and pulled him close, kissing the top of his head. "Yeah, thank you, babe. You gave me back my family."

Did you enjoy *Past Secrets Present Danger*?
If so, check out *I'm Yours*,
Book Three of the Rain City Tales.

Also by Brent Archer

Rain City Tales
The Officer's Siren (Book 1)
Past Secrets Present Danger (Book 2)
I'm Yours (Book 3)
The Wedding Weekend (Book 4)
Mitch's Men (Book 4.5)
Saving Parker (Book 5)
Song of Salvation (Book 6)
Memories of Coromandel (Book 7)
Blaze of Cortez (Book 8) – Coming in 2024

Black Rock Cult Series
Rediscovering Todd (Book 1)
Hiding Hayden (Book 2) – Coming in 2024
Dragging Marshall (Book 3) – Coming in 2025

Stand-Alone Stories
Throuple Honey

ABOUT THE AUTHOR

Brent Archer was born in Spokane, Washington, and lived there most of his adolescent life. At 18, he left for Seattle to attend the University of Washington for Electrical Engineering. Quickly, it became apparent that he wasn't wired for the required science and differential equation classes, and so he switched his major to International Studies with a minor in History. After graduation, he pursued an acting career in musical theater and dance. Once thirty hit, however, he decided to focus on numbers, getting a certificate in accounting, and became the Financial Controller of a non-profit arts and music organization.

Though writing most of his life, he never thought to submit his work for publication. In 2012, he visited his cousin Delilah Devlin in Arkansas, and she prodded him to write a story and submit it. So, he did, and it sold right away. With the encouragement of Delilah, his other writing cousin Elle James, and his husband, Brent embarked on a writing career. He's loving the journey, finding inspiration and a story everywhere he goes, whether it be the local coffee shop, driving through each of the United States, or riding the train to explore the world.

www.ingramcontent.com/pod-product-compliance
Lightning Source LLC
Chambersburg PA
CBHW070121260626
47160CB00004B/1569